# "There's someone drowning . . . !"

Two quick steps and Cord was dropping twenty feet through the air into the narrow trough between the boats. He had to reach the woman before they were both crushed.

Weighed down by his soaked clothes, his breath whisked away by the marrow-chilling water, Diamondback struggled toward the woman. Shouts came from both boats, hands reached over the side toward the woman, but she was already too far within the closing V of the steamboats. Exhausted by the cold, he managed to pull himself toward her. The boats were still moving in a loopy, drunken dance. Paddlewheels beat closer and closer to his back, closing over the both of them like the blades of a huge pair of shears. The wash was sucking at them. His numbed hands were slipping.

They were doomed . . .

*Also in the DIAMONDBACK series from Pinnacle Books*

# RIVER RACE VERDICT
## PIKE BISHOP

PINNACLE BOOKS     ◎     NEW YORK

This is a work of fiction. All the characters and events portrayed in this book are fictional, and any resemblance to real people or incidents is purely coincidental.

DIAMONDBACK #5: RIVER RACE VERDICT

*Copyright © 1984 by Raymond Obstfeld*

An original Pinnacle Books edition, published for the first time anywhere.

First printing / October 1984

ISBN: 0-523-42201-6

Can. ISBN: 0-523-43191-0

Cover art by Aleta Jenks

*Printed in the United States of America*

PINNACLE BOOKS, INC.
1430 Broadway
New York, New York 10018

9  8  7  6  5  4  3  2  1

*To Ron,*
*for pointing the way up the river*

*And to Dan Logan for*
*his assistance on this book*

# 1

"How much is the bet?" Cord asked.

"How much you got?" she said.

He poked a finger through the pile of chips in front of him. "Three hundred and twenty dollars."

She snatched up a handful of chips and tossed them into the pot. "Then that's the bet."

Cord hesitated. It was everything he had. Enough to get him out of California to safer country, someplace where he wouldn't run the risk of being recognized. Still, he had a hell of a hand. He shoved his chips into the huge pot. "Why not?"

The others had folded, but they still watched with great interest.

Slowly, Jemima Longborn spread her cards on the table. Full house, kings and deuces. She brushed the pile of chips toward her with a practiced sweep of her slim fingers without waiting to see his hand.

Cord Diamondback stared expressionlessly at the poker hand that had stripped him of his last silver dollar. Slick lady, he decided. Bluffed him silly and left him broke, but he had figured he could pick up some extra cash playing cards. And since Jemima Longborn's promised judging job had turned out to be nothing more than hired gun work, it seemed only right to take her money before anyone else's. Instead, she picked him clean.

An invisible shiver went through Diamondback. To be stuck in San Francisco, of all places, without a cent to his credit was little short of suicide.

He hadn't counted on Jemima being such a skilled gambler. But he had managed to ignore the evidence, which was all around him, of her skills: the *Clancy Longborn*'s elaborate saloon with its red velvet drapes, polished wood floor gleaming in the light of electrically lit chandeliers, and sixty-foot mahogany long bar with its brass footrail and huge mirrored wall reflecting the gleam of hundreds of shiny beer mugs. Yes, Jemima Longborn's cardplaying ability should have been no surprise.

The other two men at the table looked over at him, slight grins on their faces.

"Arthur, I think Jemima has found another true believer," said one of the men, the one dressed in a sober black frockcoat that made him look like a preacher.

Arthur only nodded and kept grinning. Both men had gone easy on the spending once they had seen which way the cards were falling.

"Broke yet, Mr. Diamondback?" Jemima asked.

"You've got it all," he admitted, pushing up from the round, ornately carved table. It was only midmorning. Quiet, except for the gamblers and a single bartender who shunted up and down the length of the bar, clinking glasses.

"You've still got leverage, you know." The woman's pale green eyes stared at him, mocking, and one corner of her wide mouth twitched upward, the corner with the thin white scar that ran along her jawline. The wide mouth had tricked him. He'd fallen for it. A hint of a victorious smile now lurked around its edges.

Diamondback nevertheless liked her mouth. And the thick, blond hair that was short, but undeniably feminine. Her tanned face showed the effects of years on the river, but the complexion was clear and cared for. Twenty-eight or thirty years old. A face that was less than beautiful, but more than handsome. Mature . . . ambitious. Diamondback liked that. Too bad she didn't have a real judging job to offer.

"The business we discussed," Jemima continued. "It could be collateral for another hand. Let's say, you win, I'll pay you two hundred dollars. You lose and you go to work for me." She looked confident as she made her offer, settled herself in the low-backed chair with a sarsaparilla at her elbow.

"No, thanks," Cord said, setting his Stetson on his head. His black eyes, deep holes, seemed to draw her frank stare and hold it.

"How do you figure on eating, Mr. Diamondback?"

"Like always." He smiled. "With my mouth." How indeed, he thought. He recalled the days when he was on the run after killing Senator Billy Fallows. Eating had been a luxury. A snake or a lizard eaten raw to avoid a campfire. He knew hunger, all right. You didn't stay hungry if you could help it, but some things were more important than being hungry for a day or two.

"You are one dumb cowboy, Diamondback," Jemima said.

Cord nodded. "I can't argue that, ma'am."

He still had a few hours to quietly scare up some money. He could take the *Clancy Longborn* to Sacramento in the morning. Get himself out of the Bay Area and back to where he could pick up his horse and gear.

The swinging doors of the saloon burst inward, almost smacking into him as he reached them.

"Jemima!" Hoodoo, the *Clancy*'s pilot, strode toward his boss without glancing at Diamondback. Cord had run across him earlier that morning. Hoodoo was about sixty, with gray stubble on his chin and wayward strands of gray sneaking out from under the short-brimmed cap he wore. "I can work magic on this river," he had boasted right off. "I'm the only one that Jemima will turn this damn boat over to. I worked for her daddy, and now I work for her. Been on this river for almost forty years."

"Jemima!" he repeated as he neared the woman. "Murkie Taggert just got throwed overboard and the man is *dead*. He decided to go into the ring against Bobo for a little practice and Bobo bashed him around for a while like he was a dory on a snag and then pitched him over the side. Ain't much left of ol' Murkie."

Diamondback turned to watch. Murkie Taggert had been scheduled to fight Bobo the Fightin' Bear at midnight tonight on the foredeck of the *Clancy*. One of Jemima Longborn's promotional schemes. The fight would bring spectators from all over San Francisco. Diamondback had seen the handbills plastered everywhere in town. Good money for the *Clancy*, what with the drinking and all that would go on. Then the *Clancy* would leave first thing in the morning on its upriver run. Cord had planned to stay in his cabin while the fight was on. No sense being recognized.

"Damn," Jemima groused. "We got people coming."

Hoodoo shrugged. "Guess we'll have to think of something else."

"Such as?"

"What about naked women? Naked women'll make 'em forget about the bear."

Jemima impatiently waved away the suggestion. "Bear wrastling's what they're comin' for, and bear wrastling's what they'll get."

Hoodoo screwed up his face in thought. "Took us long enough to get Murkie to fight him. Now Jutt Martin says Murkie went into the ring with Bobo, so he wants his money."

"He'll get his money after Bobo fights tonight. Hire somebody," Jemima said. "Offer good money. I don't care who."

Hoodoo scratched his head. "Where we gonna get somebody that stupid."

Cord smiled. "Somebody call my name?"

He might as well make a few dollars since he was stuck here till morning. The gambling losses hurt. And he had been counting on the judging job. It had been the first in a couple of months. Free-lance judges were getting fewer pickings all the time as the West developed and judges were appointed for every new state, city, and county that was created. The only jobs he got were the ones that people didn't want the law to know too much about.

So he had been over in Virginia City, Nevada, mining a little gold and picking up bar-room judging jobs. Feeling bored and useless. At the time, San Francisco had seemed a lot less threatening. Better than riding to Texas for a job.

Jemima stared at him. "You? Fight Bobo? You're afraid of what I've already offered you, Diamondback," she said coldly. "If I put you in that ring against Bobo, you'll peel up the deck trying to get under it and hide. No, I need somebody who looks as if they're *trying* to fight."

"Oh, I won't be trying to escape. I'm going to win."

The two men at the table with Jemima guffawed, and Jemima's wide mouth curved upward in a smile.

"Isn't that what you said when we sat down to play poker?"

"I'm just a born braggart. Couldn't help myself, I guess."

She studied him appreciatively. "Like the idea of that five hundred dollars, do you, Diamondback?"

"It's only money," he said, deadpan. Mentally, he was kissing each precious bill.

She kept looking at him. Handsome, with a nose that looked as if it had been busted often. Thick biceps stretched the cotton fabric of his shirt. Below the rolled-up sleeves of the shirt hung muscular forearms with tracks of long veins crisscrossing under the skin. A nice specimen. But she'd seen a lot of nice specimens on this river, good-looking men who thought they could handle the river—and thought they could handle her. A few could handle the river. Nobody could handle Jemima Longborn. "You got balls the size of Half Dome," one would-be lover told her ruefully as he was leaving. For a while that one had imagined himself becoming master of the *Clancy*. He had looked at Jemima and hadn't realized the *Clancy* already had a master.

"I'm curious, Diamondback. What's the difference between you skipping out on a little guard duty and you making a fool of yourself in front of a crowd?"

"I know I won't make a fool of myself," Cord answered. "And I don't like killing people because somebody tells me to."

"I didn't say it would be necessary to kill anybody."

"Then why hire a gunman?" Cord waited, but she didn't reply. "If I have to kill somebody, I don't want anyone telling me who it will be."

The woman's wide mouth set firm and hard, like the gash of a dry streambed in summer hardpan.

"Get the hell off the *Clancy*. *Now*."

"My fare's paid to Sacramento," he said.

"Here's a refund." She plucked a gold coin from her pile of winnings and angrily threw it at him. He caught it in midair and smiled. "Sorry, lady, my heart's just set on our little cruise." He dropped the coin on the floor, spun, and without another word he turned to leave the saloon.

"Je-*mim*-a." Hoodoo said it in the tone of a father who had been telling a beloved daughter for years to be polite to strangers.

Diamondback's steps echoed in the quiet of the saloon. His big hands spread the swinging doors.

"Diamondback."

He stopped and turned to face the captain of the *Clancy Longborn*.

"Fight Bobo the Bear, Diamondback. Five hundred dollars if you win. Two hundred when you lose. And when you lose, you get the hell off my boat. Tonight."

The white light of the winter sun glittered off the white-caps in the bay. A beautiful day, just like he remembered them.

"A thousand if I win," he said.

Jemima's wide smile lit up her face. She nodded. "I'll call your bluff, Diamondback. Bobo's going to mess that pretty hair of yours."

Cord was still smiling as he walked out, but inside he had the terrible feeling that somehow Jemima Longborn had just suckered him again.

# 2

The bear's curved black claws arced toward Diamondback's face. Diamondback snapped himself away, but the claws raked his workshirt and he felt the sharp spikes gouge trenches of fire across his collarbone. As he retreated, a loose nail in the deck hooked his boot heel and he sprawled flat on his butt on the worn redwood planking, his head rapping the hard wood.

He couldn't see anything through the yellow ball of pain that erupted from his skull like a meteor crackling across the night sky. Then he was staring up at six hundred and fifty pounds of charging bear, its black fur glistening in the light of the torches.

The bear grunted and waddled toward him, then reared on its hind legs high over Diamondback. In the cold January air it breathed misty clouds that disappeared into the thick fog of the evening as they rose.

"Attaway, Bobo, bust his ass!" Jutt Martin yelled from the edge of the whooping crowd. His fists clenched and unclenched, and his eyes were narrow slits of ugly triumph as he urged his bear on.

"Hey, Diamondback!" someone encouraged. "Get up! Hurry!"

Too late. As Diamondback tried to rise from the deck of the *Clancy Longborn*, the bear rushed forward on all fours, butting him with a broad chest that reeked of fish and sweat. A string of gluelike saliva dripped from the damp fur onto Diamondback's cheek as he was hammered to the boards and pinned. Bobo lay down on him, crushing him. Bobo's panting breath smelled of rotten fish as he stared balefully into Cord's eyes.

A hand slapped the deck three times, quickly, and Bobo pushed himself off Diamondback, not a moment too soon. The bear scrambled back toward Jutt Martin, intent on claiming his reward for winning the round.

"First fall out of three to Bobo the Bear!" cried Hoodoo, who was refereeing the match. Hoodoo hoisted a scarred fist into the air, thumbing Cord back to his corner. He followed Diamondback to the edge of the chalk circle that marked the limit of the makeshift ring. A bucket of water sat atop the hogshead barrel that was Diamondback's corner.

"Good thing he likes eatin' better'n he likes fightin', Mr. Diamondback, or you'd a been squashed like a flapjack," Hoodoo commiserated. Diamondback nodded wearily.

The men in the crowd were cheering while the women clucked sympathetically for Diamondback, obviously admiring the muscled chest revealed by his torn shirt.

Going according to plan, Cord thought woozily as he staggered to his corner, cupping the back of his throbbing head with a big hand. But his plans for rounds two and three had better work equally well or they'd be sweeping him up with a broom. "Ten thousand wins and no losses," Jutt Martin had billed Bobo. Had he, Cord, really thought he could win against the beast? Bobo's reputation for playing rough was well earned.

Come on, man, shape up, he told himself as he leaned over the hogshead. Pump up the betting.

"I got two hundred dollars that says I win," he suddenly shouted. For a moment the crowd quieted in disbelief. Then there was an uproar.

"Win, Diamondback? You'll be lucky if you can keep from gettin' kilt!" shouted an old gold miner at the edge of the crowd. The miner's pants were a half-dozen sizes too big and they flapped loosely as the old man laughed at Diamondback.

"I got the two hundred, Diamondback!" bellowed another miner in red suspenders, who waved a thick wad of bills at him. "You gonna die!" A half-dozen Chinese, their black pigtails bobbing with excitement, shoved money in his direction and chattered in pidgin.

"Dim'back, forty dollah! You lose, I bet!"

"*Fifty* dollah!"

"Diamondback, I'll bet you two hundred dollars you don't last a minute of the next round," yelled a well-dressed rancher. His money was riding high in his fist. "I'll give you two-to-one, Diamondback!"

The crowd worked itself into a frenzy of betting. He *had* to win now. He didn't have enough money to cover *any* bet.

"One minute!" shouted the timer.

Time to get on with his plan. Cord reached into the leather pack resting at the base of the hogshead. He brought out a glass jar with a metal screw cap. The jar's dark brown glass hid its contents.

Short of an obvious weapon like a gun or a knife or a length of pipe, anything went. "Bobo likes a few tricks up his opponent's sleeve," Jutt Martin had assured him with his evil grin as they set down the rules. "Keeps his interest up."

He had spent an hour that afternoon amid the teeming stalls of Chinatown. He'd quickly found three of the items on his short list. The fourth was tougher to locate, but trust Chinatown to have what was needed. A little mild haggling over price, and Cord was as ready as he'd ever be to fight Bobo the Bear.

In front of the crowd, behind a huge box camera on a thick oak tripod, hovered a photographer with slicked-back hair and a white shirt with a bright red bowtie. A vest peeked out from under his buttoned black wool coat. Eastern spiff. The crowd was giving the photographer room. Cord saw the man unleash an elbow into the mouth of an unwary spectator who had moved too close as he was changing camera plates. The victim clamped his hand over his injured mouth but made no move to protest.

A cameraman. Bad news. Cord turned himself so that the photographer would have only a view of workshirt and brown hair to play with. During the fight he'd have to try to keep Bobo between himself and the camera. Cord imagined his face spread across the front page of the *Chronicle*. He doubted he'd be recognized, but why take the chance?

The woman next to the photographer was another Easterner by the looks of her. She said something to the dude. He snarled and continued exchanging camera plates. The woman looked to be in her late twenties, with dark hair in a tight bun at the back of her head and golden eyes that seemed to pick up and intensify the yellow light of the torches.

No time for that now. He had to concentrate on the fight. The crowd was noisy and restless, ignoring Cord in favor of Bobo's antics with his bucket of fish.

Hoodoo walked over and stuck his head close enough so that Diamondback caught a whiff of the stale sweat and woodsmoke embedded in the pilot's workclothes.

"I figgered you had a little secret in mind, Diamondback," Hoodoo said admiringly.

"No secret," Cord said. With a twist he unscrewed the cap. The jar was filled with thick brown sludge.

"Whoooo-ee, smells like you kilt the meanest bear in California and put him in that jar," Hoodoo commented as he pulled back. "That is powerful bear grease."

"We'll soon find out." Cord smiled. Scooping his fingers into the muck, he began slathering it across the front of his shirt. The slick bear grease soaked into the blue flannel.

"Come on, Hoodoo, slop some of this stuff onto my back," Cord said.

The old man reluctantly dipped a hand into the jar. Cord turned his back to him. Suddenly, he felt the tail of his shirt rising. Exposing the secret of his past life.

"No!" Cord spun quickly. His black eyes flashed at the old man.

Hoodoo stood with his greased hand upraised, mystified by Cord's action. "You told me you wanted it on yer back."

"On the shirt," Cord said shortly.

"Getting a mite spooked there, ain't you, boy?" Hoodoo said coolly.

"Sorry." Cord shook himself. The old man had only been doing what Cord had asked, but for a moment Cord thought he had given himself away.

"With the shirt moving under the grease, I'll be that much more slippery," Cord explained.

Hoodoo nodded, but he was still unimpressed. "May keep you from getting kilt, but how's it gonna help you win?"

"Bobo steps on that chalk circle and he loses," Cord said.

Hoodoo's eyes gleamed in understanding. "So you figger your best chance is to get Bobo to step on that line." He snorted. "Hell, that's yer *only* chance. Gonna be a shitload easier to move Bobo ten feet sideways than it is to drop him five feet to the deck."

Cord nodded.

The bear grease sealed off Cord's sweating body from the damp winter air. With the last handful of grease, he swathed his arms and head. He had used bear grease to coat his knuckles in past fights, but he had never bathed in it. The grease smelled *bad*.

Jutt Martin had backed the bear into its corner, readying Bobo for the next round. The foredeck of the *Clancy Longborn* was the size of a big living room; its rail arced into a half circle that herded the excited crowd close together. Boys stood on the rail, teetering against the uprights in search of a better view. Diamondback vs. Bobo the Bear was the biggest event in San Francisco tonight.

Bobo snuffled around in his bucket of fish as Jutt Martin tried to get his attention by rapping his snout. Hands reached out to touch Bobo's coat. Bobo ignored them.

"Ol' Bobo likes his salmon between rounds," Martin said loudly. "Keeps his strength up!" He rolled his eyes at the appreciative crowd and grinned widely at Diamondback. Martin's two front teeth were missing, and with his long, greasy black hair and beard, Diamondback decided he rather looked like a bear himself.

"Hey, Diamondback!" a rancher jeered from near the starboard smokestack. "Let's try a little harder next round, all right?"

"Don't listen to them, Diamondback," urged one of the dance-hall girls, her frilly red silk dress partly hidden under a long black coat. "Beat the hell out of that bear. I got a hundred dollars riding on you."

One of the men called out, "Wouldn't be the first time you got money riding on a man, Tina!"

The men roared with laughter as her bright red lips rose in a leer of promise, and her rouged cheeks plumped up like ripe strawberries. Diamondback smiled at her and turned away.

"Figuring on sliding away from Bobo, eh, Diamondback?" a miner said loudly from close by.

"I'm going to grease his paws and then trip him," Diamondback replied, poker-faced.

"If Bobo falls, we're gonna have to patch a hole in the deck," Hoodoo countered. "Hell, in *three* decks."

Once Diamondback had coated his body with the bear grease, he wiped his hands clean on a rag.

"Fifteen seconds!" cried the timekeeper, and there was a rumble from the crowd.

"Five seconds!"

Bobo, as if he had a clock going in his head, was already up on his hind legs and lurching toward Diamondback. Cord barely heard the short blast of the *Clancy*'s whistle as it signaled the start of the second round.

Get in close and stay there, Cord told himself. He forced himself to move forward, dreading the thought of Bobo's rib-cracking embrace. Bobo caught him low, around the waist. Immediately, the big black bear began hugging him, and Cord felt his spine bow outward as Bobo squeezed him in his powerful front paws. The air rushed from Diamondback's lungs.

Cord fought to twist himself in the bear's grip. He needed to breathe, but it was almost impossible with Bobo squeezing his guts.

The bear grease wasn't working. Bobo had him under the arms, locked helplessly in the middle of the ring. He could slide around a bit, but not enough to throw Bobo off balance. Bobo grunted with the effort of squeezing him to death.

Desperately, Cord scratched gobs of the slimy bear grease off his shirt-sleeve with his thumbnails. He clamped both hands around Bobo's nose, forcing the balls of bear grease into Bobo's wet, black nostrils. Enraged by the grease lumps blocking his air passageways, Bobo flung himself sideways. No longer aware of the chalk circle in the terror of suffocating, the bear stepped on the line, smudging paw prints into the tiny mound of white dust as spectators scrambled out of the way. A woman screamed as Bobo smashed her into the rail in his wild dance. A bellow swelled out of the depths of the crowd. They knew it was the first time Bobo had ever lost a round.

"Second fall to Diamondback! Get that b'ar off him!" Hoodoo shouted urgently at Jutt Martin.

Grumbling, Martin boxed Bobo's ear with a salmon to get his attention. "Come on, ya big dumb son of a bitch," he yelled angrily. "Ya gettin' *stupid*!"

Huffing, Bobo pawed furiously at his muzzle, trying to dislodge the plugs of bear grease that blocked his nostrils.

"What the hell's the matter with you, bear?" Martin yelled. He poured a bucket of water over the bear's head, trying to calm it down. Bobo sneezed twice quickly and then settled to the deck, panting heavily. The water seemed to have helped.

God, it hurt, Cord thought as he slowly climbed to his feet and stumbled toward his corner. He was breathing hard, trying to make up for the eternity in which he'd gone without air. He glanced around the crowd. Most of the onlookers seemed to be enjoying themselves, despite the possibility of losing a lot of money should Diamondback manage to beat Bobo.

"Yeah, Diamondback! Good work!"

"What'd you do, Diamondback? Bite his balls?"

Cord looked around. "I get a thousand dollars if I win! Anybody willing to back me?"

Another harsh wave of noise came out of the crowd.

"Two hundred bucks for ya, Diamondback! We split the profits!"

"One hundred!"

The pair of Easterners looked amused. The photographer was working quickly and skillfully to get a picture of Bobo. "Don't take no picture of my b'ar," Jutt Martin snarled at him, then turned back to Bobo.

Side bets and counterbets punctured the cold night air. The crowd was near panic in its excitement over the possible upset. Thousands of dollars were riding on Diamondback now.

Cord's lower spine felt as if it had been crumpled. He leaned back against the hogshead, bracing himself with his elbows. The bear grease stuck like glue and Diamondback felt as if he were suffocating with the closeness of it.

"Thirty seconds!" The timekeeper's voice was high-pitched, excited. He sounded as if he wanted to help his clock move faster.

Hoodoo came up, hawking a stream of tobacco juice that spattered the deck like wet mud. "That bear grease ain't gonna work this time," he said, sounding worried.

"Have to try something else, then." Cord twisted painfully and slid a hand into his leather pack. The hand came out of the pack in a tight fist.

"What've you got, Diamondback?" Hoodoo asked excitedly.

"It's not bear grease," Cord replied.

"What, then?"

"Five seconds!"

Cord smiled at Hoodoo and pushed himself to his feet. Bobo was already on the move.

Quickly, Cord palmed the contents of his fist into his mouth and began chewing furiously. He caught a glimpse of the Easterner crouched behind his camera, and he shifted a step to his right to put the bear between himself and the photographer.

Fire suddenly pierced his tongue and in a moment turned to a raging inferno that was searing the soft linings of his mouth. Sweat broke out beneath the bear grease. His entire body seemed to leap in temperature.

"Five seconds!"

Cord's eyes began to water in torrents. His nose became a river. The fire in his mouth seemed to become a loud roaring. He could barely see the beast through his tears.

Bobo watched Cord's hands. The bear remembered the grease. A deep growl emerged from its throat and he waddled faster toward Diamondback.

The bitter fiber in Diamondback's jaw was exciting his saliva glands, producing a river of biting juice that filled his mouth. But he couldn't afford to spit it. He needed it against Bobo.

Bobo cut down Diamondback's maneuvering room quickly. With a lunge and a growl, the bear again clasped his opponent in his forepaws, and Diamondback felt the familiar painful wrenching in his spine. A gob of bear grease slid from Bobo's snout, and his mouth was open, exposing big yellow teeth.

Air. He needed air to breathe, but the bear squeezed harder.

Diamondback was blacking out. His vision started to go; he felt as if he were looking through a tunnel. In moments he'd be out cold.

The tunnel pipe of his disappearing vision centered on

Bobo's black eyes. Pressing his lips together tightly, Cord let loose a thin stream of juice, like he'd seen tobacco spitters do at a contest in Mississippi years back. A needle-like stream of the juice angled into Bobo's eyes, first the left, and then the right as Diamondback twisted his head against the bear's tightening grip.

For a second, Bobo didn't respond. Suddenly, he spasmed, squeezing Cord incredibly hard as the juice began to eat its hellish way into his eyeballs. Cord struggled for breath, and as he did, the mushy clump in his mouth was sucked toward his lungs. Rivers of juice inflamed his throat, gagging him.

Bobo was roaring as if he were trying to drive away the fire in his eyeballs with noise. Thrashing backward, he twirled Diamondback around like a bee in a tornado. Cord felt as if his head were being lifted from his shoulders.

He was blacking out. The tunnel of vision collapsed. For a moment he heard Bobo's roar mixed with the thunder of hundreds of voices. And he felt himself falling. Falling.

# 3

"I won three hundred dollars bettin' on you tonight, Cord. The least I can do is help you to your cabin," Tina said. The dance-hall girl tested his greasy arm and reconsidered the situation. "Let me pull this old coat over you. No need to spread that smelly grease around."

Tina's red cheeks and red satin dress dimly penetrated the haze that seemed to surround Cord. He limped along the deck, aching in places he didn't know he had.

"I'm going to ruin your good coat," he mumbled.

"That old thing? Can't hurt that. Besides, I'm going to buy me a new one tomorrow, in Sacramento. Got the money to get a *real* nice one. Thanks to you beating that old bear." She adjusted the top of her low-cut dress, which was drifting lower on her ample breasts. "What'd you squirt him with, anyway?"

"The finest Szechwan black garlic in Chinatown. Evil stuff." Evil was right. Cord could still feel the hot juice stewing painfully in the pit of his stomach.

Tina wrinkled her nose. "Is that what that smell is? I thought it was just the bear grease."

"I wish."

"Well, we'll get you cleaned up, somehow." She pushed

open the door to Cord's cabin and gently guided him in. "When you hit that bear with that juice, he looked like he was going to throw himself right into the bay. After he dropped you, the poor critter put his paws over his eyes and just lay there, whimperin'. I felt real bad for him."

"Me too." Cord hobbled toward the wall and leaned against it, his head almost brushing the low, open beams just below the ceiling. His back felt as if it had been twisted into a knot. Poor Bobo.

Tina looked him up and down. "You are gonna take some real scrubbing to get clean."

"Maybe not as much as you think."

She ignored his words. "Well, not much else I can do for you tonight, anyway. Got my period, you know? Won't be able to get too fancy about things."

Cord smiled weakly. He hadn't been thinking about much besides getting a good night's sleep.

Tina took her black coat from his shoulders. She sniffed as she appraised his greasy shirt. "You smell sorta like a cross between a grizzly and a Chink. Only thing gonna get that bear grease off is some vinegar."

"Just so happens," Cord said, and he slowly leaned over to where his leather pack lay. He came up with a clear bottle of white liquid.

"Vinegar?"

"Vinegar."

"You really think things through."

"If I did, I'd have figured some way to beat Bobo without going into the ring."

Tina giggled. "What have you got in there to make the garlic smell go away?"

"This." Cord produced a jar of honey. The amber liquid held a chunk of honeycomb.

Tina giggled again. "I like a man who sets out to do things *right*. I'm sure sorry I can't be as accommodatin' as I'd like to, tonight."

"We'll think of something."

"Okay, take your clothes off and lay down," Tina ordered, but Cord rummaged through another pack and pulled out a clean shirt. His back to the wall, he stripped off the greasy shirt from his muscular chest and put on the clean one.

"What are you doin'?" Tina said uncertainly, torn between admiring his muscles and wondering what he was up to. "Gonna ruin two shirts?"

"Maybe."

"Suit yourself." Tina shook her head in disapproval. "Lay down."

The bitter vinegar stripped away the film of bear grease still left on Cord's arms and neck, stinging across the cuts and scratches left by Bobo's claws.

"Now your hair. Hang your head over the side of the bed," Tina ordered.

Cord groaned. "I'm glad I didn't bring a bathtub full of this vinegar."

Tina put the washbowl on the floor under Cord's head and carefully poured some of the vinegar into his hair. The sour liquid streamed past his ears and dribbled into the bowl. Tina worked her nails through his grease-slicked hair, scooping vinegar from the pan and back onto his head.

"You won't smell of bear grease when I'm done, and you'll probably never get cooties."

Cord laughed.

"Okay, now, let's rinse that vinegar off." She poured water over the back of his head from the pewter pitcher. "If you let me take off your shirt, I'll rub you real clean."

"I look pretty good now, don't you think?" Cord asked.

"I guess you'll do," she said approvingly. "Or rather, you will as soon as we get rid of that garlic smell."

Cord carefully unscrewed the cover of the honey jar and stuck a finger deep into the sticky liquid. He quickly brought the finger to his mouth and licked it off. He ran his tongue into the nooks and crannies of his mouth, erasing the metallic bite of the garlic with the sugary honey.

"Better?"

"Sweet as a baby." Tina picked up the jar and examined it against the light. "I'll bet I can make you sweeter'n that."

"Prove it."

"Not as long as you got those pants on."

"Then take 'em off," he said.

"Now yer talkin'. Roll over and lift that butt." Tina's fingers flicked open the buttons of his fly. She tugged the jeans over his slim hips and in a moment had them off.

He stirred. His penis hardened and rose gently.

"Gettin' anxious," Tina observed. She scooped out a forefinger of the honey. Holding her finger above him, she let the thin, golden stream run onto the length of his slowly hardening organ. "Looks tastier'n strawberries and brandy," she said. "Oops." Quickly, she dived down to catch the gathering stream of honey as it reached the tip of his penis. Her tongue flicked around the tip of him and she whisked away the wayward drop. Then Cord felt her tongue working the honey along him. He stiffened.

"Whoa, boy," Tina said, giggling. Her red lips moved up the bottom side of his shaft, spreading the honey layer along his length.

"More," she said. Two fingers dug into the jar. She let

the honey run into his dark, curly pubic hair. She pushed her face in; he could feel her tongue, probing, licking the liquid from him. "Oh, baby, I'd love to be your all-day sucker," she crooned quietly. He felt her hands go under the cheeks of his butt. His hard cock slid into her waiting mouth, guided by her pink tongue, which came out to greet him.

Her warm, soft throat surrounded him and he felt the heat stroking deep inside him. He reached overhead for one of the beams. He pulled himself upward, letting his weight hang from the beam. His muscled torso stretched, tapering down to his crotch where Tina's sucking pulled on him, hard and soft and rhythmic, like quicksand.

The heat was rising in him like a bonfire stoked by a bellows. Cord thrust deep into her mouth, pushing himself in as far as he could, feeling her tongue caress him as she brought him nearer to his hot explosion.

His rib cage ached with the pull on his arms and from the residue of the pain from the fight. Suddenly, the pain and the sucking combined in a sweet ecstasy of release.

"Yeah," he breathed. Sperm jetted from him like warm honey and he could feel Tina gulping the flow of him.

Her lips squeezed against his organ, milking the last bit of him. He released a gasp of completion and lay back on the bed.

Tina licked away a pearly drop of sperm from her red upper lip and smiled. "Busy as a bee," she said.

"Come on up here," Cord invited.

"No, I've got to get out of here, Cord. Jemima catches one of us girls visiting a man's cabin, and she throws her off the *Clancy* so damn fast the poor girl doesn't have time to pull up her drawers."

"Why'd you risk this, then?"

"Now that you beat Bobo, I think you're going to be

real popular around here.'' Tina looked down and fiddled with the front of her dress. "I wouldn't have risked my job before the fight. I heard Jemima say that she couldn't wait to get you off this damn boat. She said you were a coward.''

# 4

---

The cabin door creaked. Groggy, Cord lay on the bed for an instant more, trying to figure out what was going on. Tina. Sleep. The electric lamp was still glowing dimly.

He flung himself sideways into the narrow space between bed and bulkhead, both hands readying the Smith & Wesson Schofield .45 that had rested next to his pillow.

"Excuse me. Mr. Diamondback?" A hand crept around the door, each of its fingers sporting a diamond-encrusted gold ring. "Hello?"

"Who is it?" Cord growled. The feeling of danger was ebbing. His body had taken over when his mind became too weary to function. The fight against Bobo had worn him out. Why was someone bothering him this time of night?

A face peered around the door just above the ring-studded hand. A face Cord saw earlier that day at the card table. Thin and tapered, a hatchet face with gold-rimmed glasses and topped off with an off-white panama hat that looked too large for the head it rested on. Gray hair peeked out from under the panama.

"Arthur Tellock, Mr. Diamondback. We met this morning." The older man smiled as he saw Diamondback aiming at him, ready to blow his head off.

Cord eased himself up, elbows on the hard bed, Schofield still pointed in Arthur Tellock's direction. "Tsk, tsk. Manners, Mr. Tellock. As the Chinese say, 'Knocking on door prevents bullet between eyes.'"

"I did knock. You must not have heard." The man remained pleasant, but Cord saw a flash in the dark brown eyes that said he wasn't used to being addressed so rudely. "Sorry to disturb you. I was at the fight tonight. Made quite a bit of money betting on you. Saw you fight one time up in Coeur d'Alene, and another time in Oregon. Inventive. Creative. Tonight, I figured you were a sure thing."

Cord listened impassively to the man. He hadn't heard anything worth losing sleep for.

"Anyway, since you've been good to me over the last few years, I just wanted to share some of the wealth with you. You know, as encouragement. You looked a little down in the mouth out there tonight. Not your usual enthusiasm, if that's what you call it."

"Wrestling Bobo isn't like dancing a Virginia reel."

"Decidedly not. But maybe this will help." Tellock slipped a bejeweled hand into the breast pocket of his long, off-white frockcoat, coming up with a hand-tooled leather wallet. Lots of bills. Big ones. Cord could see the hundred capping the thick stack. Tellock flicked through the crisp greenbacks with the air of someone who was comfortable handling such sums. With an audible snap of the bills, he handed them to Diamondback.

"A thousand dollars, Mr. Diamondback. I understand you prefer judging to fighting, so this might help you spread out your fights a bit—although when you schedule one, I'd appreciate hearing about it so I can plan to be there. Always like to win a bet." The guffaw he then emitted seemed louder than a body that thin could produce.

Cord stared at the offered bills. With a puff of air, he reached out and accepted the money, folding the bills over his thumb in one motion. "Thanks," he said. He leaned his head back against the pillow and closed his eyes. The bruises hurt like hell. And Bobo probably cracked a few of his ribs with those pancake landings.

Tellock was silent for a moment. "I'm a little surprised you took the money, Diamondback. Don't get me wrong, I'm happy to give it to you."

Cord opened an eye to glare at him.

"You come across as someone who doesn't want to be beholden to anybody."

"Unless you're not telling me something, Tellock, I'm not beholden to you at all. You want to give me money because I make money for you, you go right ahead." Sure enough, Cord thought. This bare-knuckle fighting wasn't going to last forever. Either his knuckles or his brain was going to turn to powder sooner or later from the constant battering. Even if he *could* dodge most of what was thrown at him. But a *bear*? What next? Crocodiles? A room full of rattlers? Shit. Better to mind his own business, stay at peace with the world as much as possible, and not have to hammer someone's brains to gelatin to make a dollar.

Tellock chuckled and waved a hand. "Diamondback, I like you. You are so *damn* unpredictable."

"Like this morning?"

"What? Oh, Jemima? Hey, that little lady is a real she-devil at poker." Tellock clicked his tongue in admiration. "Seen her skin men alive with hands you wouldn't open with."

As his mind flashed on the memory of Jemima's poker skills, Cord noticed that the diamonds on Tellock's rings were the size of peas, and cut so that they glittered with a thousand sparkles no matter which way they caught the light of the electric lamp.

"Looks like you've had some good luck yourself," Cord said.

"Yes, indeed, the wicked little turns of life." Tellock chuckled, shaking his head philosophically. "Had some tough times, though, until I got enough ahead to build up a little capital outside the gambling business."

"What do you do?"

"Well, now, it's hard to label."

"Try."

"I suppose you might call it politics. Seems as if I made enough friends—and enemies—between Sacramento and San Francisco to become quite useful to a lot of people. I deal in information. Very lucrative around state capitals."

"A little faulty information could make your life tough."

"Oh, it has, it has. Definitely a gambler's business," Tellock agreed. "But I like to bet, Diamondback. And I like to win even more. Too many years of not winning, I guess. Too long a bad streak. Can make you crazy. So every time I win, it's like the first buck I ever won. I love it."

Cord laughed. The old man seemed to relish the memory of those victories. He stood there with his gold-rimmed glasses in hand, wiping the lenses, working them absentmindedly with a silk handkerchief with the initials A.T. sewn in pale blue silk in one corner.

"Thanks for the confidence in me," Cord said. "I wouldn't get too used to it, though. Can't tell when there's gonna be a bad day. Like a six-hundred-pound bear with a hard left."

It was Tellock's turn to laugh. The thin little man replaced his glasses and stuffed the monogrammed handkerchief into his back pocket. "Well, hell, then I'll bet against you. Just let me know when the bad times are coming, okay?"

Cord smiled. "What if I need a little information?"

"What do you need to know?" Tellock asked, interested.

"Who was that photographer at the fight?"

Tellock plucked a snuffbox from his pocket and opened it. A pinch went up each nostril as he considered Diamondback's question. "He's a newspaperman from back East. Had a woman with him. Came aboard like a safari crossing darkest Africa. Lots of crates and luggage."

"What are their names?"

"That I didn't find out. Stashed themselves away as soon as they came on board. Adjoining rooms. Didn't come out until fight time. Never did get a chance to chat with either of them." Tellock sniffed. "Why the interest, if you don't mind me asking?"

"Maybe I'll get a picture of me and Bobo."

"Wouldn't be a bad idea." Tellock nodded.

"Need some proof for the tales I tell my grandchildren," Cord added.

"I hope you've got some grandchildren now, because if you keep fighting critters like that, you're not going to live long enough to see any later."

"I've been thinking of that," Cord said.

"You know, there was one thing," Tellock said, rippling his fingers against the surface of the snuffbox. "When she came aboard, the woman was examining a big sheet of paper. It was a wanted poster. She caught me looking and folded it up quick. I didn't catch a glimpse of who was on it." He sniffed again. "Be a hell of a note if she were a bounty hunter, wouldn't it? Cute little thing. Soft brown hair and eyes that are my favorite color. She could have my hide anytime."

# 5

---

"Say that again?" Cord demanded. He scratched a hand through his sleep-tousled hair. The afterburn of garlic was burrowing a hole deep in his belly like a gopher through a cornfield. No more garlic. Ever.

"Jutt Martin says you owe him for damagin' his bear," Hoodoo repeated.

Cord snorted. "Hold on one minute. Where are we?"

"Under way. Left San Francisco 'bout fifteen minutes ago. Seven hours to Sacramento. One stop."

"Okay. Now what am I supposed to have done to that bear?"

"Jutt Martin said Bobo's just meaner'n hell now. He can't manage him. Jutt said he can't make no livelihood from Bobo no more, and it's your fault."

"Bobo nearly bent my spine into a barrel hoop, and it's my fault, huh? I tell you, Hoodoo, the man has all the makings of a lawyer."

Hoodoo guffawed. "Well, I'm just passin' the word. Ol' Bobo's back there on gallery deck, pacin' and grumblin' to beat hell. Ready to rip somebody a new asshole. Jutt Martin doesn't want it to be him."

\*     \*     \*

The stern area of the gallery deck was wide open to the sky. Fog rode thick against the water. San Francisco had long since evaporated into the mist.

Jutt Martin wasn't around, and Bobo sat staring balefully astern as Diamondback approached. When he recognized Cord, he growled and angrily rose up on his hind paws. Black claws raked out at Cord. The bear's weight caused the iron cage to thump against the deck.

"Morning, Bobo."

The bear's eyes were puffy and rimmed with red. He snarled one more time and then settled back disconsolately.

It was good to get out of the cabin. He had to do some stretching. Work out the knots from the fight, particularly the sore joints of his spine. It'd be nice to have a rubdown, he thought. A woman pressing her hands hard into his back, massaging away the stiffness. But any woman who saw the braid of scars down his spine wouldn't stick around too long.

Slowly, he worked his arms, letting them pull easily at his cramped back. The cold winter air crept under his shirt and longjohns, chilling him, so he picked up his pace.

"Mr. Diamondback."

Cord turned to see who was speaking to him. It was the woman from back East he had noticed at the fight.

"My name's Chutney Crane," she offered. "I've been looking for you for a long time."

"It's a long way from Boston."

"Do I have that much of an accent?"

"The clothes help give you away."

Her leather-gloved handshake was brisk, no-nonsense, and eyes the golden yellow of browned butter stared up coolly into his own. Brown hair flowed upward at her slim neck, disappearing under the stylish hat on her head, with its ostrich feather bobbing in the wind. A thin, brown silk skirt nipped tightly at the waist was topped with a white ruffled blouse and silk jacket. In that eastern getup she had to be freezing, but she seemed oblivious to the wind.

Chutney Crane's narrowed eyes appraised him in the way a butcher might size up a carcass for dressing. The eyes flicked past the details, concentrating on the hard lines of his angular face.

"Chutney Crane of the New York *Daily Intelligencer,*" Cord said. "Notorious lady reporter."

Her small mouth smiled, but in her eyes he noted she had filed away a bit of information about him.

"Journalist, Mr. Diamondback, journalist. But I'm surprised that you've heard of me."

"I read a lot."

Her look said she was adding that tidbit to her stockpile. "Let's get to the point, Mr. Diamondback. I'm here to do a story on you. The East is well acquainted with Cord Diamondback, the West's only combination pugilist and judge. Two-fisted, six-gun justice. From your reputation, I'd guess it would make a terrific piece of journalism."

"What it makes is a terrific waste of paper," Cord corrected.

"You're too modest," she said. "There's probably half a million little boys across this country who want to grow up to be Cord Diamondback."

Cord laughed as he turned away. "I hope they don't all grow up to fight bears, or I'll go broke. Look, it's been nice meeting you, but I've got to work the kinks out of my back, okay? Bobo must have thought he was making pretzels."

"Don't let me stop you," Chutney said pleasantly.

Crouching down, Cord lay flat on his back, hooking both feet under the side rail and his hands behind his head. He began rapidly doing situps. The big shoulder muscles bulged under his shirt. Thick thigh muscles pumped against his denim pants each time he raised himself.

"Come on, Mr. Diamondback, I saw you fight that bear last night. I don't know what you did to him, but it was very dramatic stuff."

As she spoke, the man who had been with her the night before appeared in the stern stairwell. A heavy box camera on a tripod was draped over one shoulder, while his other hand carried a big wooden equipment case.

"Who's he?"

The reporter glanced toward the stairs. "That's Clay Gibbs. My photographer. I'll introduce you." She waved a hand. "Clay? Clay, come over here and meet Mr. Cord Diamondback." She turned back to Cord. "He wanted to shoot a few more pictures of Bobo, but since you're here we can get some of you with the bear."

"I don't want to get any closer to Bobo than I am right now."

Something flashed in the golden eyes. Something Cord couldn't read.

"Don't be shy, Mr. Diamondback," she soothed. "The camera won't steal your soul, if that's what you're worried about. The Indians seem to think a camera will steal their souls when the picture is taken."

Gibbs had placed his camera and equipment carefully on the deck and walked over to where Diamondback was doing situps.

"Clay Gibbs, Mr. Diamondback," Chutney introduced. "Mr. Diamondback is hesitant about having his picture taken."

A tiny sneer crossed the young photographer's face. "Think of it, Mr. Diamondback. All your friends will see you." It was standard photographer's cajolery, but Gibbs said it cynically, as if that would be all it would take to convince his subject.

"Typical photographer. Arrogant and self-centered. And crazy about camera equipment," Chutney said, trying to smooth over the photographer's rudeness. "He brought a boxcar full of stuff, I swear. New inventions, he says. He rambles on."

"That one uses dry plates," Gibbs said proudly, hooking a thumb in the direction of his camera. "New development. Easy to handle."

"It was developed ten years ago, in England," Cord said.

"How do you know that?" Gibbs said.

Cord shrugged. "Met the guy who invented the process."

"Well, if it interests you, you won't object to Clay's taking the pictures," Chutney Crane said brightly.

"No pictures," Cord repeated.

"Clay." Chutney Crane threw a warning glance at the photographer and he flushed. Without another word, he walked away.

"I need your picture, Mr. Diamondback, and I want an interview with you," Chutney said seriously. "You're the reason we came out here."

"Should have cabled me. I'd have saved you the trip." Cord finished his situps and unhooked his feet from the rail.

"But the *Intelligencer* felt your story was worth pursuing. My editors felt that you symbolize a certain segment of life in the West."

"What segment is that? The bear fighters? From the quality of what you call the 'journalism' in the *Intelligencer*, I'd say it would read more like a pack of lies," Diamondback said. He moved to walk past her, but she quickly stepped in front of him and placed a gloved hand lightly on his forearm.

"It's not as bad as all that. Besides, from what I understand, you'd prefer to do more judging and less fistfighting. With a little boost from the *Intelligencer*, the whole country would know about Cord Diamondback's legal skills. You could build your own courthouse and have your clients come to *you*."

Cord shrugged off her hand and dropped to the deck. His hands almost touching, he began doing pushups. He was still breathing heavily from the situps.

"Don't you ever quit? How many of these things do you do?" Chutney flared impatiently.

"Depends."

"On what, for God's sake?"

"Well, it's about six more hours till we reach Sacramento."

"I don't believe this," she grumbled. "Mr. Diamondback, I think you'd better take a break for a while."

"Why?" The pushups were coming harder now. The blue veins in his thick forearms throbbed steadily as he slowly forced himself all the way up. Arms quivering, he let himself down until his nose almost touched the floor.

There was a click from behind Bobo's cage. Cord glanced to his right. The photographer was atop the pilothouse deck. He had just snapped a plate shut in the big camera, which was pointed at Cord. A satisfied expression rode Gibbs's face.

"I want to talk, Mr. Diamondback." Quickly, Chutney crouched next to him and spoke quietly. "I want to talk about Christopher Deacon."

# 6

Sharply sucking in his breath, Cord pushed. Slowly, the muscular body rose off the deck like a boom lifting a shipment of bullion. His trembling arms fully extended, he held himself rigid for a long moment. Then, suddenly, he snapped his legs under his body and he was standing. His warm, panting breath came out as puffs in the damp air.

The *Clancy*'s twin stacks chuffed loudly and rhythmically, pumping black smoke into the gray mist. White foam trailed behind the boat as it headed northeast, away from San Francisco.

Cord turned his back to the photographer, putting his elbows on the rail as he spoke. "Seems to me I said I didn't want my picture taken. I knew he'd get my bad profile."

"Have you ever been to Boston?" Chutney asked.

"Been to Boston," he said. "But I spent more time in New Bedford, when I thought I wanted to be a whaler."

"Senator Billy Fallows was killed with a whaler's harpoon," Chutney said.

Cord's face snapped toward hers, his eyes cold and depthless, like those of a snake about to chomp on a mouse. "And my initials are C.D., same as Christopher

Deacon's. And no, I won't show you my back. I've been through this before, Miss Crane.''

Chutney laughed suddenly. Her words surprised him.

''I remember when I was about thirteen, listening to Patrick Sarsfield Gilmore's orchestra. You should have been there. The whole of Boston turned out for the spectacle. His orchestra had one thousand pieces, and there were ten thousand voices in the chorus. The topper was the fifty firemen hammering anvils for the anvil chorus in the *Meistersinger*. My girl friends and I thought we would simply die laughing. It was *so* funny. And there's my father standing there looking as if he were listening to St. Peter's own choir welcoming all of Boston to the pearly gates.''

Cord *had* been there, had heard Gilmore's orchestration of church bells and the ringing anvils. Chutney was right; the event had been absolutely hilarious, even more so because he and some Harvard buddies had been drunk at the time and had all but fallen off their perches laughing.

But that had been another world. Now he was Cord Diamondback.

Cord Diamondback. A little too flamboyant, perhaps. The initials a mistake. A name that attracted attention, even when the man didn't. Not a name for a wanted man to hide behind. Particularly when only a thin layer of cloth stood between him and exposure as one of the West's most wanted criminals.

How much of a man was in his name? As Christopher Deacon—the name suggested a sobriety, uprightness, piety—he had indeed driven a harpoon through the fat bag of corruption that called itself Senator Billy Fallows. Without regret. Certainly not the mark of saintliness. Simply a necessary job, the vengeance of a man with little left to lose. And now he gazed at Chutney Crane, waiting to hear in which fateful direction she was going to shove his life.

"Anvils. Can you imagine?" She was letting him drift on the treacherous seas of doubt and dread.

"Seeing my father standing there enraptured by that horrible noise . . . I mean, I'd have expected that of Philadelphia, but in *Boston*?" She stared smugly at Cord. She was playing with him, testing.

"No wonder you left," he said.

She laughed again. "Isn't that ridiculous, a lady journalist hailing from Boston Brahmin stock? My parents were mortified when I announced I wanted to become a journalist—my father less so than my mother—but the idea of me trotting around after stories . . ." She shrugged. "So I moved to New York City, got a job at the *Intelligencer*. My first big story was 'A Night in a Brothel.' I wrote it first-person, about what it is like to be a whore. I did a composite character from the women I interviewed, I really didn't do any such thing myself. But because it was first-person, everyone assumes I tried it out."

"Run out of town, right?"

"I am now officially *persona non grata* in Boston, although my father keeps in touch. He believes in me."

"He'd better. Looks as if you're pretty determined."

Gibbs's camera plate clicked again and Diamondback glanced up at him. Gibbs removed the exposed plate and slid it into a holder bracketed between the legs of the camera's tripod.

"Clay doesn't know who you really are," Chutney said quietly. "But he's a bulldog when it comes to getting pictures. He had a real hard time getting a photograph of you at the fight, and he's determined to make up for it today."

Cord considered the gray mist enclosing the *Clancy Longborn*. "Well, what the hell," he said. Then he snapped his fingers as an afterthought. "One thing, though. If you're so convinced that I'm Christopher Deacon, my picture should be worth some money to your paper."

"I'm sure the *Intelligencer* would make it worth your while," Chutney said quickly.

"Five thousand dollars ought to cover it."

"Five thousand? They want your picture—not to own you outright!"

"I need something for my trouble. And if you identify me as Christopher Deacon, I know there will be plenty of trouble."

"For five thousand dollars, I want to see your back."

Cord smiled. "For five thousand dollars, you can see anything you want."

The golden eyes stared up into his, trying to read his bluff.

"I'll have to cable back East for the money."

"*Now* you're talking. Let's take some pictures." Cord spun and strolled toward the bear.

"I want to see your back," Chutney insisted.

"Cash up front on the back," Cord said. "We might as well get these pictures now, though. I'm getting cold." He looked up at Gibbs. "What do you want me to do?"

"Get up close to that cage and talk to Bobo. As if you guys are enemies inside the ring, but buddies outside it."

"That bear'll try to rip my throat out," Cord said doubtfully.

"Well, just get as close as you can and we'll see how it goes."

"I'll try." He stepped toward the cage. With a growl, Bobo rose on his hind legs. Reaching through the bars, he swiped at Cord. By instinct, Cord leaned away. The claws missed by an inch. Bobo had a longer reach than he thought.

"Beautiful," Gibbs enthused, snapping the exposed plate out of the camera and into its holder. "Try it again."

Cord puffed up his cheeks as if he were going to spray some garlic juice at the bear and Bobo went berserk, ramming both paws out toward his former opponent in a futile attempt to snare him. As Diamondback backpedaled, Bobo gave a roar of frustration that boomed out into the fog. The bear dropped to all fours and lumbered around the small cage, rattling it against the deck.

"Look, I've got an idea," Cord said. Quickly he made his way around the cage until he was just below the spot where Gibbs had stationed himself on the pilothouse deck. Reaching for the lip of the deck, Cord hoisted himself upward. "I'll crouch up here, just over Bobo's cage. You back up and get a shot of me with Bobo looking up at me."

As Cord clambered over the edge of the upper deck, his knee slipped. Frantically, he flailed out, struggling to keep himself from falling onto Bobo's cage. His wildly grasping fingers caught the heavy leg of the camera tripod. Cord tried to pull himself forward, but the weight of the equipment wasn't enough to hold him. He dropped backward, taking the camera with him. As he hit the deck, the bulky camera and its tripod arced overhead, smashing into the barred roof of Bobo's cage with a jangle of breaking glass and twisting metal.

With an angry roar, the beast clawed at the camera, tearing furrows in the leather bellows. Seizing a tripod leg in both paws, Bobo ripped the equipment through the bars of the cage. The camera broke apart as he thumped it across the bars like a stick run along a picket fence. More than a quarter ton of angry bear stood on the exposed film plates, which popped like firecrackers before falling silent. Then Bobo picked up the film plates and flung them out of the cage. They sailed into the sky like black metal crows, tumbling end over end before they splashed into the water.

Cord picked himself slowly from the deck. Arching his back, he worked his head around on his shoulders. The fall had hurt. "My God, I'm sorry," he apologized. "I'm stiffer than I thought. I—"

Angrily, Clay Gibbs vaulted off the pilothouse deck. "You did that on purpose!" he shouted. His teeth were bared and his hands curled into hard fists.

Gibbs was taller and heavier than Cord, and he had a long reach. A hard right poked out at Cord, clipping his cheek. Blood sheeted down Cord's face where Gibbs's ring caught him.

"Stop it, Clay!" Chutney shouted. "It was an accident!" But the photographer moved in as Cord reeled backward against the rail.

"I'll replace it. I'll take it out of the five thou—"

Gibbs threw a looping right that Cord blocked. His own right came from the knees, digging hard under Gibbs's rib cage. The easterner exhaled a gust of air and snapped forward. He fell to his knees, struggling to catch his breath.

"What are you doing!" Chutney cried. Anxiously she looked from one man to the other. "Are you going to kill each other over an accident?"

"Five hundred dollars' worth . . . of equipment, Diamondback," Gibbs wheezed. He was still on the deck, clutching his chest. Drops of sweat beaded and dropped onto the deck as he squeezed his eyes shut in pain.

Calmer, Cord looked at Chutney Crane. Arms crossed, she glared at him.

"My, my, Mr. Diamondback, you certainly must have something interesting tucked away in that past of yours." As if she didn't know. Her eyes sparkled flecks of gold.

"When you get the five thousand, you'll find out."

"Minus five hundred."

"Accept my apology and make it five thousand."

"You won't get the money if you try to trick me," Chutney said.

"You're paying for the examination. No money, no examination."

"I'll want some more pictures. Along with the interview."

"You have to have the pictures? Every tough guy west of the Mississippi is looking to start a fight with me," Cord groaned. "If they know who they're looking for, I'll never get any rest."

Chutney laughed. "My heart bleeds for you, Mr. Diamondback, but the price includes a few shots of you and Bobo."

Clay Gibbs had recovered enough to straighten up.

"Are you all right, Clay?" she asked.

Gibbs growled and spit at Diamondback's feet, but made no move to rise.

"I give you the money. We take a look at your back, get a few pictures, and do the interview. Then you can disappear into the hills, or whatever it is that you two-fisted western free-lance judges do when your work is done."

Her eyes were unreadable. Was she baiting him? Would she have him in jail by nine A.M.? He doubted it. If she believed he was Christopher Deacon, she'd poke and prod until she could milk every bit of drama out of it that she could. A real journalist.

She dismissed him with her smug smile. "Till later, Mr. Diamondback."

# 7

"You want your thousand dollars, I suppose," Jemima said.

"Sure do."

Jemima had glanced at Cord as he stepped into the *Clancy*'s pilothouse, and then she returned her attention to the featureless fog ahead. Hoodoo was poking around through the grate of a stove near the port side of the room-size cabin.

Visibility was less than a half mile, Cord guessed. There was something way off to starboard that he couldn't quite make out. Shore, probably.

"I've got to admit, Diamondback, I didn't think you'd beat that bear. Even bet fifty dollars with Hoodoo. He said you'd win."

Hoodoo cackled with glee as he peered into the grate. "I figured with my savvy and his muscles, he had a chance. Didn't realize he brought some savvy with him."

"Where'd you learn that garlic trick?" Jemima's pale green eyes flicked over him again.

"Rodeo riders juice up their bulls that way. If they get a ride that's a little too peaceful, they give it some encouragement."

"No wonder those poor animals are so ornery."

The *Clancy*'s pilothouse stood open to the chilly winter air. Jemima wore a leather coat scarred from flaming embers from the *Clancy*'s stacks. Standing next to the wheel, which was taller than she, Jemima seemed oblivious to the weather.

"When does this fog usually break?" Cord asked.

"It's still closing in," Jemima replied. "Got me worried. The *Westerner* will be coming downriver toward us. We won't see her till she's right on us." She reached up and tugged on the whistle lanyard. The screech of the steam rolled away and was swallowed by the fog. "You're going to have to wait till we get to Bell Ridge for your money, Diamondback."

"No problem."

"What was that little ruckus back there?" Hoodoo suddenly asked. He stopped jabbing at the fire to stare pointedly at Cord. "I figured you had enough of Bobo for one trip."

"It turns out that Bobo's interested in photography. He tried out the man's camera."

"Is that what was going on?" Hoodoo chortled and hawked a stream of tobacco juice into a can near the stove. "Well, I don't mind tellin' you, that photographer feller earned it. That boy made some enemies last night. No need for all that hittin' and elbowin' people just to get a picture. No need for it at all."

"He seems to think so."

"Damn Easterners are all alike," Jemima said, not moving her eyes from the water ahead. "Wish they'd go back East."

"Maybe they're going by way of Sacramento," Cord suggested. If Chutney Crane was sure who he was, and if she was arranging to have him jailed, Jemima would be in on it.

"They didn't say much, except they wanted pictures of the fight. They're snobs," Jemima said. She tugged on the whistle lanyard.

No sign of tenseness in her. The wide mouth was set in a firm line. If Chutney had a plan for capturing him, Jemima didn't know about it. But he had already learned about her bluffing skills the hard way.

"You should interest them in the *Clancy*," Cord said. "Biggest sidewheeler on the Sacramento. Two hundred forty feet long. Thirty-foot diameter paddlewheels, with eight-foot buckets. Built for speed *and* comfort. That should appeal to them."

"Not bad," Jemima said, impressed. "You seem to know a lot about the *Clancy*."

"Not really."

Jemima's eyes checked the compass and then rose to the black water ahead. Hoodoo leaned to the engine-room speaking tube. "Ty, how's it goin' down there?" he shouted, and he pressed his ear to the tube. Apparently satisfied, he gazed forward into the fog.

The polished rosewood wheel rocked gently in Jemima's hands as she made tiny corrections in their course.

"My daddy, Clancy Longborn, owns this boat. Daddy holds himself very highly, which is why he named the boat after himself." Jemima's thick blond hair ruffled as she shook her head in disapproval of her father's egotism.

"I thought he was dead."

"I don't believe it," she said.

"Most people seem to."

"Well, a lot of people don't like my daddy," she said. "He bounced from steamboat to steamboat for a long time before he managed to buy the *Clancy*. He had his own ideas about being captain, and sometimes they didn't square with the owner's ideas. So he'd be out of a job.''

Hoodoo cackled happily, now that the ice in Jemima's voice seemed to be breaking up a tad. ''Yer daddy was the best Sacramento River pilot there ever was, but he liked to do things *his* way. Every boat he piloted, he seemed to think he was the owner. Remember when he hung Taft Stanford over the tail end of his own boat because the man wanted yer daddy to race at Grappa Shallows?'' The grizzled face swung from Jemima to Cord. ''Her old man spent three months in jail on that one. Only got out because Stanford drowned himself on the same stretch of river, trying to do what he tried to get Clancy to do. So they let Clancy out of jail. Figgered he had been doing Stanford a favor and the guy was too dumb to realize it.'' Hoodoo chuckled again and continued. ''But her daddy was a crazy one that way. Never did get it through his head that a boat wasn't his.''

''People like him, though,'' Jemima interjected. ''Think he's peculiar, but they like him.''

''How did he get the *Clancy*?'' Cord asked.

''Bought it cheap from J. K. Barber of all people,'' she answered. ''She had her bottom tore out—she was called the *Folsom Queen* back then—and Barber figured she wasn't worth the scrap price. Figured Daddy couldn't do anything with her, anyway. But Daddy got her a bottom and put her back on the river. Daddy *was* always kind of impressed with himself, and he liked a good joke, so he named it the *Clancy Longborn*, just to piss off Barber, mainly. And it did, because the *Clancy* is the *Westerner's* sister ship, a little bigger than the *Westerner*—that's Barber's boat—and just as plush and pretty. And people liked Daddy, so he took a lot of business away from the Sacramento

Steamboat Company. No matter what Barber and his buddy Senator Fallows tried, they couldn't—''

"What do you mean, Senator Fallows?" Suddenly Cord was listening intently to the woman. She looked over at him, puzzled by his intensity.

"Senator Billy Fallows. He was in cahoots with Barber. Hell, who wasn't Fallows in cahoots with? He and his political machine tried to force Daddy off the river. Might have done it too, if Fallows hadn't gotten himself killed. When I heard the news, I just laughed and laughed. I don't like seeing people get killed, but Fallows was no man, he was a *snake*."

"So Barber can't touch you now?"

Jemima laughed bitterly. "Oh, Barber touched us all right. He wants *everybody* off the river. And he's doing it too. Why, just in the last three months, the *McCool* blew up in a race across Suisun Bay. They figure somebody knocked out the engineer and threw a whole barrel of oil into the boiler. There were pieces of the *McCool* scattered clear to Vallejo, they said. But since the *McCool,* the *Blaze* sank in San Francisco Bay, the *Alaska* lost both paddles up in the delta, and they found Mike Gilley stabbed in the gut and tied to his wheel—they spreadeagled him, shoved his cap down his throat, and killed him."

"How do you know it was the Sacramento Steamboat Company?"

Jemima shrugged.

"Seems as if you don't have much evidence."

"You're right. Which is why I brought you here."

"I box and I judge. I don't do detective work. Get Pinkertons."

"I can't pay Pinkertons."

Cord leaned his six-foot frame against the bulkhead.

"From what I hear about your father, he could just as easily have gotten drunk and fallen overboard."

"Bull!" The muscle in Jemima's jaw worked angrily. Her knuckles were white on the rim of the wheel.

Hoodoo looked at her sadly. He squirted a jet of tobacco juice into the can in the corner before speaking to Diamondback. "Her daddy was ready as the next man to take a few snorts too many of whiskey, and that night Jemima was handling the boat. He figgered the *Clancy* was in good hands, so why not tip back a few. He may have been drunk all right, but if he went overboard it was because somebody baled him up in a roll of barb wire and tossed him over. Her daddy hated the *feel* of water. Anybody who smelled him could tell you that. Drunk or not, he wouldn'a touched water long enough to drown in it."

Cord laughed.

"You know, Diamondback, I called you yellow the other day when I was angry," Jemima began. "Now I've had time to think about it. And I still think you're yellow." She reached up and yanked hard on the whistle lanyard, sending a screech of steam bellowing out into the fog. "Bobo or no Bobo, you are chickenshit."

Cord straightened, his black eyes flashing like two chunks of hard coal on a sunny day.

"Because I'm not going to go to war with the Sacramento Steamboat Company for you?"

"Because you haven't even proposed an alternative. I simply want to keep the *Clancy* on the river and make my living. I don't care if the Sacramento Steamboat Company gets rich, as long as they leave me alone. And as long as I don't find out for sure that they killed my daddy."

Cord was silent, thinking about her words. She was right. Since returning to San Francisco, he'd felt as if he'd been trapped in a bad dream. All the old memories—the sharp, shiny harpoon slicing easily through Billy Fallows' fat belly, the helpless anger of knowing his father and brother were dead, murdered, the fear of knowing he might be recognized and captured at any moment—yes, he'd been swathed in memories, barely aware of what was happening around him.

Jemima looked at him, raising her voice as she noted his lack of attention.

"They told me you were a judge who managed his decisions so that they *had* to be followed. You've got a reputation for action. Which is more than I could get in any court between Sacramento and San Francisco. So I decided you were right. I came up with an idea. All you'd have to do is judge the result."

"What do you have in mind?"

"A race."

"The *Clancy* against the *Westerner*, right?"

She nodded, surprised. "If I win, they leave me alone."

"And if you lose?"

"I'll run the *Clancy* up on a bank and set fire to her."

"What makes you think they'll leave you alone even if you beat them?"

"That's what I'm hiring you to figure out."

The damp air boiling through the open wheelhouse sent a shiver coursing through Cord's battered body. The cobwebs in his head seemed to clear. It'd feel good to do the work he wanted to do—even here near San Francisco, where it was dangerous for him. He was a judge—if not the legally approved version, still he believed in justice and the way it should be enforced with everything in him. Ironically, he, a "murderer," had committed his "crime" in the name of justice.

"Consider me hired."

Hoodoo chuckled victoriously, but he kept his eyes on the sea, not looking at Diamondback or Jemima.

Jemima didn't say anything. Her face remained as expressionless as if she were holding a royal flush with a thousand-dollar pot.

Cord surveyed the choppy water that vanished into the fog. "How do you keep from running this thing aground?"

She still didn't say anything.

"The *Clancy* can skim over a heavy dew," Hoodoo filled in. "Her daddy got her so far off course one night in the fog that we had to send out scouts in the morning to find the river again."

Cord laughed.

"Listen," Jemima ordered.

They listened. A faint chuffing came to Cord, easily mistaken for the *Clancy*'s engines, but slightly different in rhythm and pitch.

"The *Westerner*," Hoodoo said.

Jemima nodded. "Big, single stack. Running too fast for this fog." She peered forward into the mist, then pointed. "There she is."

A quarter mile ahead, a steamboat as big as the *Clancy*, single stack flaring black smoke, was pushing their way.

"It's the *Westerner*, all right. Her pilothouse is flush with the bow. Makes her look like a dredge, if you ask me. She's also running opposite our schedule. J. K. Barber wasn't able to run me off the river by going head to head with me, so he switched the *Westerner*'s schedule. He leaves Sacramento when I leave San Francisco."

"Sounds as if it should work out fine for both of you."

"The railroads get most of the traffic now," she said. "Leaves me with not quite enough business. Fewer passengers waiting for me. And Barber always has his crew try something. You'll see."

The two steamboats raced toward each other. Cord felt the deep rumble of the *Clancy*'s steam engine, heard the sidewheels slashing through the water. Up ahead, the *Westerner* drove forward—directly in the *Clancy*'s path.

"Who moves over first?" Cord asked.

"I do. Barber can afford to sink his boat. I can't. I can't afford to pay for any damages either. So I simply move over." As she said it, she swung the big wheel to starboard and the *Clancy* edged away.

For a few moments the *Westerner* seemed content to maintain its course. Then it corrected to port, so that it was once again aimed at the *Clancy*.

"Standard procedure," Jemima remarked. "Barber's men like to scare the hell out of my passengers before he finally gets out of the way."

Sure enough, the few idlers leaning over the bow of the *Clancy* were getting ruffled about the oncoming steamboat.

"Hey, Captain, ain't you seein' that boat up ahead?" a man in a mackinaw shouted nervously.

"I'm seein' him," Jemima called.

The onrushing wind was cold, and Cord hunched his shoulders against its bite. "When do they usually back off?"

"Close enough to throw a little fear into us. He's on my side of the river, so he can't afford to get too cute or he'll be in jail, even if he doesn't kill anybody. 'Course, if he doesn't kill anybody, his buddies in Sacramento can cover for him."

The *Westerner* held its course and didn't appear ready to budge.

Jemima reached up and tugged the whistle lanyard. The screech ripped the air. "C'mon, you bastards, move over," she muttered, concentrating on the oncoming boat.

"How close do they usually cut it?"

"Ten, twenty feet. Gives the passengers a thrill. They don't seem to think there's any danger. They think I'm up here in total control. Instead, I've got a moron who's bearing down on me and I don't know what his problem is, or what he's going to do." A trickle of sweat ran down her temple from under the warm thatch of blond hair.

Then the other boat turned into the *Clancy* a few more degrees.

"Damn," Jemima hissed. "I either give in to him and dig up some bottom, or I stay on this course and hope they dodge us. Hoodoo, get those people off the bow."

Hoodoo bolted out of the pilothouse, yelling at the fascinated passengers.

Cord kept his mouth shut. If anybody knew the river and the opponent, it was Jemima Longborn.

There was no room left to maneuver now. Whatever happened, it was going to be a tight squeeze.

"I don't believe this," she muttered. "Why are they risking their own boat?" She was upset now. "And look at those fools on deck," she said, nodding to the lower deck of the *Westerner*. "They're laughing and having a good ol' time like this was part of the fare. Goddamn."

The *Westerner* plunged toward them. Diamondback could make out the faces in the wheelhouse.

"That's J. K. Barber himself!" Jemima suddenly exclaimed.

Then it was too late to talk.

# 8

---

"No way, Barber. This is all you're getting!" As she shouted into the wind, Jemima turned the *Clancy* minutely away from the *Westerner,* reluctantly bargaining for one more inch of clearance. The *Westerner* rumbled to port of the *Clancy.* If she stayed on her present course, she and the *Clancy* would smash together somewhere along their stubby curved bows. Aboard the other boat, J. K. Barber's fat cheeks bunched in anger. His pilot's horror-stricken face seemed frozen in the little square windowpane that framed it.

With twenty yards separating the onrushing boats, Barber said something and the pilot of the *Westerner* frantically tried to swing the boat away from the *Clancy.* Sluggishly, the *Westerner* responded. The *Westerner* began to swing away, but the movement was agonizingly slow. Diamondback found himself gripping a beam overhead to save himself from the jolting impact.

Jemima leaned forward, watching as the *Westerner* rushed by. "He's gonna—"

Suddenly, Diamondback was slammed against the bulkhead as the sound of timber scrubbing against metal tore the air. The *Clancy* twisted sideways, toward the other boat. People were screaming aboard both boats.

The bow of the *Westerner* was wedged tightly under the *Clancy*'s overhang. The gap between the two boats scis-sored closed as the paddles of each boat thrashed the water madly. The paddlewheels smashed together and tortured metal suddenly squealed without let-up.

"Shut them down, shut them down!" Jemima was yelling into the speaking tube to the engine room. A cut over her eye bled steadily as she struggled to bring the *Clancy* under control. The paddles were still turning. If they weren't shut down quickly, the two boats would chew themselves to bits.

In the gap between the two boats, a flash of frilly white caught Cord's eye. A woman's hand! Frantically, the hand clawed at the *Westerner*'s smooth metal hull, vainly clutch-ing for safety.

"There's someone overboard!" he yelled.

In the confusion, no one else saw the woman, who was going to be sucked into the *Westerner*'s damaged paddle as it beat itself against the hull.

Two quick steps and Cord was dropping the twenty feet through the air into the narrow trough between the boats. He had to reach the woman before they were both crushed.

Weighed down by his soaked clothes, his breath whisked away by the marrow-chilling water, Diamondback strug-gled toward the woman. Shouts came from both boats, hands reached over the side toward the woman, but she was already too far within the closing V of the steamboats. Exhausted by the cold, Cord managed to pull himself toward her. The boats were still moving in a loopy, drunken dance. Paddlewheels beat closer and closer to his back.

Got her! His powerful fist grabbed the woman's coat midway down her back. He lifted her head above water. Blood ran from both nostrils, leaving pink streams along the pasty-white face.

"That's my wife! Merry! Merry!" someone shouted desperately from above them. "Save her!"

The two steamboats continued to slip past each other toward destruction. The gap between the boats closed over Diamondback and the desperate woman like the blades of a huge pair of shears, the deafening slap of the paddles echoing hellishly in their ears.

Despite her struggling, the woman was safe in Cord's strong grasp, but the *Westerner's* port paddlewheel loomed overhead. They were doomed.

Desperately, Cord reached for the bent framework of the paddlewheel housing. He missed. Then a mighty effort pulled him and the woman against the hull, but the flashing paddle was only a foot away from them as its broken blades waggled crazily through its endless circle. The wash was sucking at them. His numbed hands were slipping, but he could no longer "feel" them sufficiently to make them grip harder.

Then the wheel seemed to slow. With a last clatter of splintered wood, the *Westerner's* portside wheel disengaged.

Cord slipped into shock. The shouts around him sounded muddled and distant. Someone pulled the woman from his grip.

Then, hands grabbed his collar and he felt himself floating into the air that seemed a thousand times colder than the river. His teeth began chattering.

"Somebody bring some blankets!" he heard Jemima order. Feet pounded on the deck. "Wrap them up. Quick! Get them near the fireplace in the main salon!"

Cord opened his eyes to a forest of faces as hands lifted him.

"You'll pay for this, Jemima," someone shouted.

"Go to hell, Barber!" Jemima returned. "Eli! Get some

boat hooks. See if you can break us loose before I go over and kill that son of a bitch!''

"You're going to be okay, Mr. Diamondback," one of his bearers said. "You're just a little damp, that's all."

"That'll teach me to try to walk on water."

"Well, rest easy for a little bit and see that everything's working. After that fight last night, we want you in good shape in the future so we can do some betting on you."

"Why, have you got plans for me to wrestle a steamboat?"

"You've already done that. You won."

They gently sat Cord in a chair that had been pulled close to the big fireplace. The fire began to penetrate his frozen skin, and steam began to rise from him.

"Somebody get those wet clothes off him," Jemima said.

"No!" Cord growled, and clutched his shirt. He couldn't let them see his back or they'd throw him back in the river.

"All right, all right," Jemima said, looking perplexed by his refusal.

The woman whose life he had saved was lying on the floor under a pile of blankets, being attended to by her husband.

"Oh, Merry, Merry, Merry," he crooned as he held her white hands. "You're going to be all right, Merry, you're just a little cold." The woman's eyes fluttered, then stayed closed.

Crouched, he turned to Cord, not letting go of his wife's hands. "Thanks, mister. In all the excitement, I never saw my wife fall overboard. I'd go crazy if she died."

Cord shrugged under his blankets. "Pure luck I saw her."

"This is insane, a collision in the middle of nowhere," the man said. "What kind of fools are operating these boats?'' He shook his head. ''I'm sorry, Mr. Diamondback. Look, if there's any way I can help you out, just let me know. My name's Curtis Blaine.''

Diamondback nodded, embarrassed. ''I'm ready for a change of clothes,'' he said. The onlookers made way as he moved toward the door.

''Very impressive, Mr. Diamondback. The dime novels understate your, um, good qualities. A genuine hero.''

He turned. Chutney Crane stood examining him, a slight smile on her face. ''You should have at least let the captain get those wet clothes off you.''

''Couldn't. No underwear. After all, how would it look?'' Cord said, and turned away from the reporter.

Jemima peered over the side of the *Clancy* at the damage. ''The son of a bitch sheared off part of my sidewheel,'' she complained. ''Look at him, though.'' They had managed to separate the two boats. To Diamondback, the damage to the *Clancy* looked minor, a number of broken paddle buckets, but no structural damage. The *Westerner* had borne the brunt of the collision. The ten-foot-high paddle that drove her forward on her port side had been shredded by the wheelhousing that protected the *Clancy*'s paddlewheel. A carpet of broken wood littered the river behind the *Westerner*.

''If he bent his walking beam on that side, he's not going anywhere,'' Jemima said.

''That'll keep the bastard out of our hair for a while,'' Hoodoo said. He whistled in satisfaction.

''We can make it to Bell Ridge,'' said Jemima. ''They didn't twist any heavy metal, thank God. I'll remember that when I take a swing at him.''

''Was anyone hurt?'' Cord asked.

''Mrs. Blaine is okay. There's some cryin' going on

among the women. Glass cuts, bruises, but nothing serious. Not like we hit head-on.''

"What will you do next?"

"Keep on going, after we get the *Clancy* fixed. The *Westerner* is worse off than we are, she may be laid up for a while with any luck. It's my chance to scoop up Barber's traffic and get it aboard the *Clancy*. Long as they don't bring the law into it, get me shut down. But they'll try.''

Jemima pushed her mouth up close to the speaking tube. "Let's go, Ty.'' After a moment, Cord felt the slam of the drive gears engaging. The paddles began turning and the *Clancy* slowly began to move forward. Jemima spun the big wheel to starboard.

"Have to correct for the damaged paddles,'' she said, pulling on the whistle lanyard. The steam screeched in what sounded to Diamondback as a forlorn sort of triumph. "Ol' *Clancy*'ll be as good as new tomorrow, after a little work in Bell Ridge.''

"Little sluggish on the uptake right now, ain't she, Jemima?'' Hoodoo noted. "Reminds me of this old boat I was on thirty years ago. We called her *Leapin' Lena*, cuz to stop her we'd have to dump an old leather coat into the gears. And to get her started towin' a load, we had to get a flyin' start, and when that load hit, it'd about jerk your head off yer shoulders. Got so's yer neck didn't know which way to snap.''

Cord laughed, but Hoodoo's story didn't pull Jemima out of her gloom. "Quit jawin', Hoodoo,'' she said. "Keep an eye on that port wheel.''

"Trouble with Jemima here,'' Hoodoo said, addressing Diamondback after a moment, "is that she's got her daddy's high regard for herself, but she lost a little of his sense of humor. And you need a sense of humor on this damn river.''

"That Barber is a crazy man," Cord said.

"Syphilis," Jemima said.

"What?"

"Barber has syphilis," she repeated. "If you get up close to him, you can see it. His nose is rotting away. Here." She pointed to the base of her nostrils.

"I take it the syphilis is beginning to affect his brain."

"Seems to be. I mean, he and his thugs are responsible for what's happening on the Sacramento, the murders and all. But Barber has gotten really creepy since my father disappeared. They say even his own men are afraid of him because he flies off into rages. Does strange things for no reason."

"Like what?"

"Well, I heard he gouged the eyeballs out of a puppy on Nob Hill one day. Just poked his fingers in, spasmlike. The dog belonged to the wife of the head of the San Francisco water district. One of his own cronies. They said he stood there with his hands all bloody and the dog yelping and crying, and he didn't even seem to notice what he was doing. Somehow, he hushed it up. But syphilis or no syphilis, Barber is dangerous. I sure don't like the idea of having to berth near him in Bell Ridge."

# 9

"There's the son of a bitch now." Jemima glared toward the *Westerner*, which was lying alongside the dock fifty feet astern of the *Clancy*. Three men were tromping down the *Westerner*'s gangway.

"That's J. K. Barber in the green," Jemima said. "Behind him, looking like the thug that he is, is Cheat Grimes—guess how he got his name? And the last guy is Burly Crawford. Longshoremen. Barber's bodyguards."

Cheat Grimes was at least six-three and he seemed taller in the black hobnail boots that carried him across the dock in Barber's wake. Burly Crawford was half a foot shorter than Grimes, and wider, like the sawed-off stump of an old redwood. Both wore holstered six-shooters whose barrels poked out from beneath their wool coats.

Now Barber was more than just an angry face in the *Westerner*'s pilothouse to Diamondback. The man was big. Six-two, two hundred twenty pounds, maybe. A thick belly bulged under the dark green vest under his open coat. No different from any well-dressed, well-fed San Francisco businessman.

Except for his walk.

Barber seemed to stagger along. Both hands drifted

away from his body, and he kept his legs wide, as if to keep himself from keeling over at any moment. The right foot dragged each time as it came around. Behind him, the man Jemima had identified as Cheat Grimes had an arm out as if he were ready to grab his boss under the arm if he began to fall.

"Look at him," Jemima said in disgust. "No wonder he tried to ram me. He's drunk!"

"He's not drunk," Cord corrected. "It's the syphilis. He's pretty far along, I'd guess. The disease is eating away more than just his nose. Looks like it's chewing through his brain."

"How long can he keep that up?"

"Few more years, maybe. He'll get more and more out of control."

The main street of Bell Ridge ended just above the dock where the two steamboats were tied. As Barber shambled toward town, he happened to catch sight of Jemima and Cord on the stern of the *Clancy*'s promenade deck. He halted, turning slowly to look up at them. His head bobbed on his shoulders like a whiskey bottle floating in a choppy ocean.

"Longborn! Longborn! How long can you keep this up?" His voice was flat and nasal. "You're trying to kill us all, woman! One way or another, you will kill all of us!"

Barber's eerie cries echoed through the hollow created between the river bluff and the two big steamboats. Passengers on the dock began to edge away from this man shouting strange things at the captain of the *Clancy Longborn*.

"If I kill anybody, Barber, it'll be you!" Jemima shouted back, but the man didn't seem to hear as he gazed vacantly into the sky over their heads. Then things seemed to snap back into focus for him and he staggered with the sudden clarity of it.

"It's an ugly thing you women do to us!" Barber raved. "Never ending. You, Jemima Longborn, know what I mean!"

"He's crazy," Jemima said. She looked uncomfortable. Women on the dock were becoming nervous. Wives moved closer to their husbands, whispering to urge them to leave the dock more quickly.

Cheat Grimes put a hand on Barber's shoulder and said something to the man. Like lightning, Barber swung an elbow back, catching his bodyguard in the ribs. Grimes backed away but continued whispering urgently to Barber.

Staggering, Barber twisted himself toward Bell Ridge and hoisted himself up the slope without paying any more attention to the scene around him. As Grimes and Crawford lumbered along after Barber, their faces turned toward the *Clancy*. Crawford said something as Cheat Grimes raised his index finger toward Jemima and Cord. Then they were gone, lost behind the huge piles of coal and stacks of cordwood piled behind the rough wooden buildings of Bell Ridge.

"That man scares me," Jemima said with a shudder. "He hates me."

"I'm not sure it's you he hates," Cord said. "I think he hates women. For being the cause of his syphilis. With his mind going, he has focused all that on you, I'd guess."

"What can I do about it?" Jemima said in desperation. "If his mind is rotting away, even if I win a race against him, it'll only make him hate me more."

"Doesn't matter at this point," Cord said.

"Why not?"

"He'll keep trying to destroy you, race or no race. If

you race him, you stand a chance of improving your situation. Your original idea was a good one."

"But what if I win and he doesn't give up?"

"Chance you'll have to take. But that's why you're hiring me. To enforce the decision."

"Can you do it?"

"Have to get him to agree to the race first."

Cord moved. With a glance at the Smith & Wesson Schofield .45 holstered on his hip, he headed for the *Clancy*'s landing stage.

"Where are you goin'?" Jemima demanded.

"To work."

"Well, you tell Barber he's payin' for the repairs on that paddlewheel."

Cord didn't respond. He'd be happy simply to get Barber to agree to a race, he thought.

"Did you hear me, Diamondback?"

"I heard you."

The main street of Bell Ridge reminded Cord of bigger cities. Buckboards lumbered up and down the dirt streets with their loads of crops being delivered to the railroad for shipment east. Bell Ridge hummed with the rising energy of a small town confident of its future. As the midway point between Sacramento and San Francisco by water, and because it was a stop on the Central Pacific's eastward route, the town was a stopover for every traveler between the two cities.

The town was built on the side of a gentle hill. Uphill from the pier, Cord could see the "good" part of town, the small band of whitewashed houses that overlooked the river and its rough commercial buildings. The main street was a mishmash of civilized and half-civilized structures, the older ones left over from the last rush for gold ten years before.

Barber and his men were walking down an alley paralleling the river. Cord guessed they were making for the boat yard to see about repairs. The *Westerner* had been towed into Bell Ridge a good hour after the *Clancy* hobbled in.

Cord turned into the alley. In a few moments the men ahead disappeared under a worn sign that read O'NEILL'S SHIP SUPPLY. From behind the barn that served as the store, Cord could hear the sound of hammering and sawing and the thumps of lumber being dropped to the ground.

He pushed open the door and stepped into the store. The four men standing there turned. The conversation stopped.

"Whaddaya want?" Cheat Grimes demanded. Apparently he recognized Cord. J. K. Barber held a length of coarse rope in his hands. It was tied in a hangman's noose. He turned from his conversation with a man in a leather apron and stared at Cord.

"Who are you?"

"I seen him hangin' around with Longborn," Grimes interrupted before Cord could speak. "I saw 'em on deck a few minutes ago when we were coming up here."

"Yeah," Burly Crawford confirmed.

Barber's dark eyes looked as if a black cloud had suddenly passed between them and the sun. His nose was fleshy and crisscrossed with jagged blue-red veins. Cord could see the messy sore digging into the man's upper lip. The madness that had gripped Barber on the dock seemed to have passed. There was a tremor in his movements, but he seemed to have regained his grip on himself.

"If he's been with that river whore, get him out." Barber lurched backed toward the man in the leather apron.

Grimes and Crawford stepped toward Cord.

"I've got a business proposition for you, Barber," Cord said.

Barber ignored him, and Grimes reached out a meaty hand for the front of Cord's coat. "C'mon bud—"

As Grimes pulled Cord toward him, Cord drove his knee upward, catching the bigger man wide open. Grimes stumbled sideways and dropped to the dirt floor with a groan of pain and surprise.

Burly Crawford's right hand was already dropping toward his gun. Cord dived toward him, catching him at the waist and sending the bodyguard careening into the counter, which splintered under the force of his fall.

"Hey, what is this!" the man in the leather apron exclaimed. "What the hell are you doing? Get out of here!"

Barber surveyed his two men, the men who were supposed to protect him, lying groggily in the dirt.

"Hold on a minute, Gus," he said, putting up a hand to slow the store owner. "Now, who the hell are you?" he said to Diamondback.

"My name's Diamondback. I was aboard the *Clancy* this morning."

"You were the one who rescued that woman." Barber ran a fist over the bridge of his big nose. "You shouldn't ride with Longborn. She'll kill you."

"Long as you're determined to get in her way, I guess she might."

"My dream . . ." Barber looked down at the noose in his hand. Slowly he worked it around his fist so that the loop ran just behind his knuckles. "My dream is to loop one end of a long line around the taffrail of the *Westerner*. And loop the other end around Jemima Longborn's neck." He snapped the noose tight. "Then I'd see how fast she could swim. Just get her out there behind the *Westerner* and tow her to San Francisco and back."

"Wouldn't count on getting the opportunity, Barber."

Cheat Grimes eyed his cohort Crawford, and Cord saw Grimes's hand inching toward his gun. Suddenly Cord's Schofield was in his hand, centered on Grimes's chest.

"Don't." Cord returned his attention to Barber. "Jemima asked me to come down here to maybe work something out between you two."

"She did, did she?" Barber smiled, and the caked sore under his nose looked like a mustache.

From where he sat on the dirt floor, Cheat Grimes bellowed a laugh. "Diamondback, huh? A goddamn Indian."

Barber's eyes softened their focus. He seemed to drift away. "There's nothing to be worked out. Clancy Longborn wouldn't cooperate. And then he sent his daughter to contaminate us, to prey on the men of this river."

"That's why I'm here. To offer you your chance to get her off the Sacramento."

"How is that?"

"A race to Sacramento. *Clancy* against the *Westerner*. Winner gets the other boat."

Barber's thick fingers dug into his coat pocket as he thought silently. He took out an ivory toothpick and inserted it between his thick lips, working it around with his tongue so that the toothpick bobbed like a rattlesnake's head.

"My boat's down because of her."

"We both know you'll have it fixed by midnight."

"How do you figure?"

"That wheel was still spinning free when it tried to take my head off. A badly bent shaft would have frozen it."

"Smart man. What part do you play in this?" Barber asked, flicking the ivory toothpick with his tongue.

"I set up the rules, make sure they're enforced, and render the decision."

"What do you get out of it?"

"A thousand dollars from each of you. Win or lose."

"What if I don't like the decision."

"Well, hell," Cord said. "If you agree to the rules, then you're agreeing to a decision. You're paying me to set the rules and enforce the decision."

"Who says I need you, Diamondback? I can keep the law out of this, and I can still get that whore off the river."

"Maybe. But you caused a real ruckus, ramming the *Clancy*. There are some mighty unhappy passengers walking around. This way you can clean things up quick. You get the *Clancy* off the river, then if anyone complains about today's set-to, you just have to tell them it won't happen again. Like you said, with your friends helping you, that should be enough to smooth any ruffled feathers. Might not be so easy if you and Jemima Longborn continue to butt heads."

The ivory toothpick danced beneath Barber's draining sore. "Got it all figured."

"That's what you'll be paying me for."

"And I suppose Jemima has already slipped you enough to enforce the right verdict."

"How long do you think I'd be in business if my decisions had a price?"

"I don't know how you managed to stay in business this long, mister. Even if your decisions are good, you have to collect your money."

"I enforce my decisions and I get my money."

"How?"

"I manage."

Barber laughed hoarsely, but his beady eyes bored into Cord's, sizing him up. "What kind of rules you got in mind?"

"Simple. The two boats leave together. First one past Sandy Bar wins."

"And we'll run at night?"

"If it's agreed to. Why waste time?"

Barber whistled around his toothpick, but he seemed unconcerned. "Racing at night on the river." He snorted and shook his head again. "Whaddaya think, boys?" Barber laughed to his men. Burly Crawford's stupid face looked confused, as if he were trying to puzzle something out.

"Never mind," Barber said quickly. "Okay, Diamond-back. Eleven tonight we meet. I'm getting Jemima off this river once and for all. Her and her old man have been nothing but trouble. Time to finish it."

"J. K., what the hell are you talkin' about?" Burly Crawford piped up.

"Shut up," Barber said. He turned away from Cord. "Now get out of here and let me get my boat repaired."

Cord backed out the door of the ship's supply, holstering his gun as he did. He trotted back down the alley toward the *Clancy*.

Something was up. If Barber was making plans to get rid of Jemima tonight, his agreeing to the race wouldn't make any difference one way or the other. He, Cord, would have to warn Jemima to post some guards.

But Barber's irrational hate for women troubled him. Barber was striking out at his imagined enemies. And he was aimed right at Jemima.

# 10

"Mind if Jemima and I talk alone for a bit, Mr. Diamondback?" The man wearing the silver marshal's badge stared hard at Cord as if trying to push him out of the pilothouse with his eyes.

Opposite the marshal, Jemima stood with her wide mouth set in a grim line. "No need for Cord to leave, Harmon."

"Suit yourself." With a last glance at Cord, Harmon Brake turned back to Jemima. Brake was Cord's height, but ten or twelve pounds heavier. Forty years old, maybe, with a black mustache and beard. He wore a white ruffled shirt and black four-in-hand bowtie with a black broadcloth coat and a bowler.

"Understand you people had a little set-to on the river this morning," Brake said. "Some of your passengers weren't too impressed." He showed his teeth in a leering smile. Big yellow teeth seemed to leap out at them.

Jemima waited.

"I thought I'd come over and find out what you people are up to."

"Not much, Marshal. Just sitting around shooting the breeze, waiting for you to come over so's I can buy you a drink." Jemima flashed an insincere smile at Brake.

"What were you doing out there?" Brake growled.

"I was on my upriver run, minding my own business, and Barber tried to run me over. If I hadn't turned toward the shallows over there by Turnip Flats, he'd have hit me head-on."

"Foggy out there, wasn't it?"

"Hell, yes, it was foggy, but we still had five hundred yards visibility. The man deliberately turned into me. The only fog is in J. K. Barber's head! The man's crazy!"

"Some of your passengers said you were going pretty fast, considering there was so much fog."

Jemima snorted. "If you'd asked them earlier, they'd have said I was going too slow to get them to Sacramento on schedule."

Outside the pilothouse, the sun had broken through the fog and Cord could see blue sky overhead. Brake was acting like a man in over his head. As if he had come over with the intention of humbling Jemima and suddenly found the barrel standing on its wrong end. Like any coward, he had a big ladleful of the bully in him.

"Seems to me this is getting to be a game to you and Barber," Brake said, scratching his beard. "Two, three times a month you two are out there playing footsies in your riverboats."

"Now I suppose you're going to give me your bushwah about women not being meant to be riverboat pilots!"

"Don't get heated up, Jemima," Brake cautioned. He looked at Cord as if to enlist him on his side. "This woman doesn't need to be out on the river, but she gets all feisty when somebody makes a joke about it."

"Seems like it's her business," Cord said.

"Joke? You couldn't tell a joke if a bear was chewin' on your ass! When you're the only woman pilot on the river and you have people refusing to ride your boat because a woman is piloting, you tend to lose the fun in it," she snapped.

Brake shook his head in frustration. "I'm going over to see what Barber has to say. I see that you're both going to be here for a while, fixing these boats, but don't plan on leaving Bell Ridge until I tell you to. Until I'm satisfied that people's lives aren't in danger because of you two, I want you to shut down."

"I've got shipments due in Sacramento," Jemima protested. "I can't be hangin' around here—hell, I'm far enough behind schedule as it is, because of Barber."

"Tough, sister." Brake raised a warning finger. "You don't move this boat, got it?"

Jemima lowered her voice. "I'm moving half a million in currency for Wells Fargo. Cash to buy gold. They won't be pleased, Marshal."

Cord watched Brake's face. The man's beard rippled as he clenched his jaw, considering the position he found himself in.

"Better arrange to have it moved by railroad."

"It'd take a day and a half to arrange. I'm supposed to have it at the Rio Vista dock by morning."

"The railroad will get it there."

"Wells Fargo'll be real pleased to hear that, Marshal."

Cord sidled over to the stove and poured some coffee into a thick white mug. They were both doing some bluffing, but Cord couldn't tell who was winning. Or what the stakes were.

"Seems every time you stop in Bell Ridge for more'n five minutes, you cause me trouble," Brake complained. "Jes' like yer daddy."

"If I stay for five minutes, you try to hold me up for a day," Jemima snapped. "The railroads are faster'n me already without you helpin' 'em."

Brake colored and glanced at Diamondback. Cord busied himself with the view.

"Well, you don't move until I say. And I'm going to tell Barber the same thing. You two think you own this damn river. I'm going to let you cool your heels until I find out what happened."

"Great. Just great."

With a last glance at Cord, the marshal stepped out of the pilothouse and worked his way along the hurricane deck.

"Damn him," Jemima swore. "He has been a pain in me and my daddy's rear ever since I can remember. Told him I had Wells Fargo money because that's the only thing that keeps him off my back. First of all, he don't want to piss off the railroad. Second of all, he don't want to piss off anybody else with the money to help him along. Like Wells Fargo. He isn't sure if I'm lyin', but he can't take the chance."

"What'll he do?"

"Listen to the passengers. Try to build enough of a case to get a grand jury going against me. He won't *really* tackle Barber because of Barber's friends."

"Does he take money?"

"More'n I can afford."

"I've never heard of this guy before," Cord said.

"Aw, Harmon Brake has been a marshal around here ever since I kin remember. Until the railroads came in he was no more trouble'n a fly on a horse's ass. Then he hooks up somehow with the Central Pacific, and suddenly he's Mr. Bigshot. He even proposed to me once and I told him to go to hell. Since then, he's had it in for me and Daddy."

"What has he done to you?"

"Not much, really. He's mostly too chickenshit and too

lazy to do anything. He'll hold us overnight once in a while. Check our shipments. Lookin' for stolen gold, he says. He's just reporting it to the railroad, though. He's shown more gumption since the railroad got ahold of him. I think they're booting him in the butt pretty hard. He *has* to do somethin'. He'll probably get a bonus when he gets me 'n Barber off the river so's the railroad can step in.''

"Jemima!" It was Hoodoo, bursting into the wheelhouse. He was panting. "The passengers are all down in the saloon. They want to see ya. Don't look like no Sunday-go-to-meetin', either.''

"Great," Jemima said. "I'm trying to get this boat patched up, and instead I feel like a preacher flapping his jaws on Sunday morning." She grabbed her coat and headed for the door of the pilothouse. "Let me get the passengers taken care of and the repair work going, and then we'll talk about Barber. I can't afford to lose many passengers these days, or Barber won't even have to win a race to get me off the river.''

# 11

---

Diamondback saw Jemima frown as she pushed through the batwing doors of the saloon. Many of the steamboat passengers—particularly the more prim and proper married women—had never seen the inside of a saloon before. Whatever drove them in here today was not likely to be good news for Jemima.

A rumble went through the crowd as they noticed her, and then they quieted expectantly. Glasses continued to clink along the bar.

"Afternoon."

Mumbled greetings came from the front rows. People toward the rear of the crowd pressed forward, intent on being close enough to hear the goings-on.

"Afternoon, Jemima," Arthur Tellock said comfortably. "Thank you for coming down." The gambler was dressed as carefully as he'd been the night before when he visited Cord's cabin. His suit and panama hat were gray today, but the same diamond-covered furnishings sparkled in the weak sunlight that filtered into the saloon.

Tellock pulled over a chair and rested himself in it comfortably. A snuffbox appeared in his hand and he pinched a fingerful in each nostril before proceeding.

"Jemima, many of your passengers feel that several issues must be resolved before we continue on this trip. They have appointed me spokesman for the group—on a purely friendly basis, you understand—to present the questions concerning the remainder of this voyage. Actually, there are two issues. First, we'd like to know *when* we will reach Sacramento. That is, *if* we will reach Sacramento. I—"

"Of course we'll reach Sacramento," Jemima interrupted, her green eyes flashing. "I expect to leave here at midnight and be in Sacramento by three A.M."

"We hear there's going to be a race between the *Clancy* and the *Westerner*," Curtis Blaine shouted from the middle of the crowd of passengers, overriding Arthur Tellock's attempt to continue. "We've already had one close call. Are you willing to get all of us killed?" Blaine was red-faced, angry. Cord guessed that seeing his wife go overboard had set him to thinking, and soon he had stirred up many of the other couples aboard the *Clancy*.

"Where'd you hear about a race?" Jemima asked Blaine.

"Couple of goons from the *Westerner* started spreading the word a little bit ago," Blaine replied. "The same two who were with that madman who was shouting at you. They said the two boats are going to race tonight, and that we'll probably be killed if we stay aboard the *Clancy Longborn*. And I, for one, agree with them!"

"Yeah, what's goin' on?" came a small chorus of cries from different parts of the crowd.

"Why should you figure on being killed?" Jemima demanded.

"Who hasn't heard about riverboat racing? We've all seen the papers over the years. What do you take us for, fools? My wife and I are leaving. You've nearly killed her once already. Do you want to make sure you kill her next time?'' Blaine was working himself into a frenzy. His delicate rodentlike face was flushed and his wispy blond mustache twitched and quivered.

Jemima's face reddened. The thin scar along her jaw showed white.

"We've all heard about the race," Arthur Tellock put in, sniffing in the juices that the snuff had loosened. "I for one am looking forward to it. Should anyone care to place a wager on the outcome of the race, I'd be more than happy to accommodate him."

"You're crazy, Tellock," Blaine accused. "If the boiler blows on this thing, we'll all be burned to death."

"The boilers aren't going to blow," Jemima said flatly.

"Even if they don't, you've got that maniac over there who's willing to crash into us and kill us all before he'll quit!"

"That's true," Jemima admitted. The look on her face said she had reached a decision. "I agree with you. It's dangerous. However, it's my last chance on this river. I don't blame those of you who want to leave. I'll refund the fare of anyone who wants to get off the *Clancy* here in Bell Ridge. I'm sorry for the inconvenience, and I hope you'll be back in the future. But unless I see this through, there won't be any future for the *Clancy*. And I'm damned if I'm going to let J. K. Barber run me off this river!"

"Attaway, Jemima!"

Her passionate speech brought cheers from the men along the bar.

"I want you people to stay aboard the *Clancy*," Jemima continued. "If you want to leave, fine. But the next train won't be here till morning. We'll be in Sacramento before then. And everyone rides free from here to there."

Another cheer went up. Jemima's offer met with the crowd's approval, but Cord listened to nearby conversations.

"Hell, Mary, it might be fun. We're in no real rush to get to Sacramento," one older man just ahead of Cord whispered to his wife. "Yer damn mother is more dangerous than any old steamboat boiler."

"The gambler's right. Ought to be real interestin'!" spoke up a bleary-eyed miner at the bar who was pouring a shot glass of whiskey into his beer. "Hey, Tellock, I got twenty dollars says the *Clancy* will beat hell out of the *Westerner*!"

"You're on," Tellock said.

"Fifty on the *Clancy*!" someone else shouted.

Tellock pointed a finger at the bettor.

"You're all crazy," Curtis Blaine shouted. "No wonder steamboats are disappearing from this river—there are a bunch of madmen in charge!"

Blaine and his wife made their way toward the door of the saloon. Many others, mostly couples, followed.

"We can't afford to die, ma'am," said one plain, workworn woman who touched Jemima's shoulder. "We've got seven children at home. I'm sorry. You seem like an honest lady."

Jemima smiled wearily. The woman patted her shoulder and left.

Cord made a rough count of heads. They'd lost about half their passengers. About a hundred, maybe more, remained.

Chutney Crane and Clay Gibbs were still in the bar. The journalist worked her way through the drinkers to Cord.

"Do these riverboat races occur often?"

"They used to," Cord said. "Back in the fifties and sixties there were a lot of them. Which is why riverboats have almost killed themselves off. A lot of people became afraid to ride them. And a lot of others liked the excitement. Thousands of people would line the shore to watch a race."

"I can see why," Chutney said. "It does have sort of a primitive appeal, racing through the night at top speed against your number-one enemy in the world. I like it." She nodded to herself. "Well, keep yourself alive, Mr. Diamondback. Don't ruin my story." The reporter clicked away with her photographer in tow.

Jemima sagged against the wall near the entrance to the saloon. Cord walked over to her.

"What's the matter?"

Her green eyes were glistening. "Those people leaving are the ones I'm trying to keep. I'm no hell-raiser, like my daddy is," she said. She talked about him as if he were still alive. "I love my daddy, but I don't want to be like him. And I don't want to run a boat the way he does. People think he's funny, but they don't trust him. I don't want that kind of reputation."

"You don't have much choice other than to go through with the race."

"I know."

Tiredly, she pushed herself off the wall. "I've got to go give refunds," she said, and walked out of the bar.

The remaining passengers seemed to have banded together more closely as a result of their decision. The drinks began to flow more quickly as new friendships began to develop.

"Hey, Tellock. You gonna ride the *Clancy* and bet agin' her? Shit, we'll throw you overboard to lighten the load!" bellowed another gambler in a frockcoat worn shiny with age. "You and all these Chinks. Chinks don't weigh as much, though, and we may need 'em to paddle!"

"Hell, I don't care who wins, as long as it's me!" Tellock shouted. "But I got to admit, Jemima Longborn's a lot prettier than J. K. Barber, even if she walks around like she's got a weasel up her ass!"

The crowd laughed.

Turning to Cord, Tellock hoisted his shot glass in a kind of salute. "Jemima's the exact opposite of her daddy. Ol' Clancy would be figuring ways to wedge those valves to squeeze a few more pounds of pressure out of those boilers. Clancy's *destiny* was to blow himself sky high, not drown like a rat. But Jemima . . ." Tellock clicked his tongue. "She'll live to be a crusty old lady. That damn little woman just might be a success on this river. She sure don't know how to have fun, though. Sure as hell hope she doesn't blow us all to hell."

# 12

---

"Are you ready to tell me what Barber said?" Jemima demanded.

"Seeing that you've been pretty busy, I figured it could wait," Cord replied.

Wrench in hand, Jemima raised her head and stared at him impassively from the skiff where she was overseeing the repair of the *Clancy*'s paddlewheel. She leaned her weight into the wrench as one of her crew tightened the nut on the inner side of the paddle.

"Okay," the crewman said.

Jemima relaxed. "Keep at it," she said, handing him her wrench. With another scan of the wheel she muscled the skiff alongside the *Clancy*'s main deck rail and clambered up.

The crew's sledgehammers whacked against the iron framework of the paddlewheel with a steady clanging that echoed through the dusk. Cord leaned against the rail and watched the progress of the repairs, although the endless hammering irritated him. Why should he stay aboard the *Clancy*? He had a thousand—no, almost two thousand— dollars in his pocket, and he didn't need the judging job. So why should he wait around for Chutney Crane to expose him? But the challenge of maneuvering Barber into the race sparked something in him. Barber wasn't going to make it easy. The risks might be too great, though. Like a mouse picking at a piece of cheese in a trap, Cord might press a hair too hard.

"Talk," Jemima said.

"He agreed to a race. Figures he'll be ready by midnight. We'll meet at eleven."

"Good."

"He was a little too quick to go along with the idea," Cord said. "Maybe he has something planned between now and then."

"I'm tempted to beat him to it," Jemima replied. "Me'n the boys could raid the *Westerner* right now. Put her on the bottom permanently." She was serious.

"Right. And Barber would have you all in jail before the *Westerner* hit bottom."

She was just blowing steam.

"Well, we're going to work until this is done," she said. "That paddle will be rebuilt by midnight. Maybe earlier."

Her fist tapped gloomily against the splintered wood of the paddle. "I've listened to more griping today than I've heard in twenty years on this river." She shook her head and the blond hair waggled listlessly. "I didn't try real hard to get out of the way."

"If you had given the guy the river, he'd have wanted the shore," Cord said. He rose to go.

"Thanks for saving Mrs. Blaine, Diamondback," Jemima acknowledged. "Don't need a death on my boat. The railroads have bitten deep enough into my business without me handing my passengers to them."

"Bell Ridge probably appreciates the extra business. You should be able to get some action out of the townspeople tonight."

"Either Barber will or I will," she said, but she brightened a little at his words. She glanced in the direction of the *Westerner*. "J. K. already cut the price of drinks tonight."

"I don't think he's going to be worried much about drinks. I'd keep your eye out." Cord began to walk away.

"Where are you going?"

"Get some sleep. Gonna be a lot to do later."

A sneer curled Jemima's lip.

"You should get a little rest too," he advised.

"I can make it, Diamondback."

He shrugged and walked away.

"Why, Mr. Diamondback. Just the person I'm looking for." Chutney Crane approached Cord as he stopped at his cabin door.

"I thought you'd be out getting pictures of the damage," he said.

"Clay's heading that way right now," she said. "Once he quit fussing about your, um, clumsiness, he became quite excited about the whole riverboat thing."

"At least he's got a better subject."

"I wanted to suggest that since we seem to have so much time available this evening, we might do our interview then."

"Why don't we just skip it?"

"I suggest we explore Bell Ridge a little bit. We can talk at the same time." The golden eyes were confident and there was that hint of a smile on the small mouth. The eyes promised something Cord was not quite sure he wished to know.

"Are you going to have the sheriff pick me up here?"

Her light laughter was muffled by the *Clancy*'s thick carpet. "I'll only have you arrested if you *don't* make a good story. Above all, what I want is a good story—better yet a series of good stories. Or best of all, *one* story that will make me the best-known reporter in America. I mean, I want everybody from San Francisco to Boston—especially Boston—to know the name Chutney Crane.''

"Marvelous."

"No, Mr. Diamondback, look, why does this have to be so difficult? We go out tonight, we do the interview. God, it's boring here. What do they do for fun out here in the boonies?"

Cord ignored her, letting himself into the small cabin. "Did you wire for my five thousand dollars?"

"Mr. Diamondback, you are *so* unromantic," Chutney said, following him into the cabin. "Yes, I wired for the money. It will be waiting in Sacramento. Now what about the interview?"

"What about Gibbs?"

"Oh, he won't be there. He became quite sulky when I told him I was going to interview you and didn't need him along. He says you're dangerous."

"He's right."

"I hope so, Mr. Diamondback." Again her eyes flirted with his and Cord found himself looking forward to the interview.

"How about a deal?" he offered. "I'll ask the questions, and I'll answer them. You listen and take notes."

Chutney frowned. "Not much of a deal. Certainly not for five thousand dollars."

"Then we could skip the pictures and skip the cash."

The golden eyes scanned his face, and then her small mouth widened in a smile. "I'd rather pay the money."

"Ah," Cord said. "Then let's get to work."

Chutney was looking around the cabin, absorbing details. Cord's bedroll and soft leather pack lay on the floor in one corner, next to the chair where his wet clothes were drying. Atop the small chest of drawers were papers soaked from their trip into the bay.

"I didn't think you'd want to go so quickly," she said. "I'm not dressed."

Cord watched as the woman edged toward the papers, trying to get a glimpse of what was there.

"Find anything interesting?"

"What? Oh, excuse me," Chutney said. She flashed him a coy look. "I'm sorry. Force of habit." She moved away from the papers.

Cord smiled. "For Bell Ridge, you look fine the way you are. Besides, we won't be in Bell Ridge for long."

"Oh?"

"I'd prefer to talk where there's a bit more privacy."

"Sounds perfect. Where might that be?"

"Trust me."

"Do you trust *me*, Mr. Diamondback?"

"Only when I have you in sight."

"Then it should be a very pleasant evening for both of us."

"Going to get some sleep, Diamondback?" Jemima asked dryly as he walked toward the landing plank with Chutney Crane. The two women sized each other up, Jemima taking in the newspaper reporter's eastern dress and makeup, while a little twist of Chutney's mouth gave away her opinion of the other woman.

"You haven't met Captain Longborn yet, I take it," Cord said. "Captain, this is Miss Chutney Crane of New York. Miss Crane is a journalist. She's here to do a story on the West's only woman steamboat captain."

Chutney twisted toward him, but her denial died as she realized what he said. The story possibility snagged her.

Like a voracious shark attacking a whale's carcass, she would rip away flesh until she had stripped a subject of its story possibilities.

"Mr. Diamondback is right, Captain. I think the story would make our readers sit up and beg for more. Particularly if there's a chance she'll wind up going down with her ship. Er, boat. Do you call the *Clancy Longborn* he or she?"

Jemima snorted, but Cord could tell she was intrigued by the attention, reluctant as Chutney Crane seemed to be to provide it.

Chutney breezed forward. "Very nice meeting you, Captain. I'm sure we'll be talking soon, once the boat is underway again. Is every trip this, um, melodramatic?"

"Sure is," Jemima said. Her green eyes glittered in the light of the torches used on the outside of the *Clancy*. "Fact, things are a little dull so far. We'll work on it, though, if we're going to be in the papers."

"I'm sure you will," Chutney concluded, and continued on, the high heels of her stylish black boots thumping in a rapid staccato on the wooden deck. Cord followed.

"Diamondback."

He looked at Jemima.

"You've got a funny way of getting a job done."

"What's the problem?"

Jemima's wide mouth worked its way into an angry frown. "The second these two boats are ready, I'm leaving. And I wouldn't mind leaving without you."

# 13

"I think the lady has—what do they call it out here?—a hankerin' for you Mr. Diamondback," Chutney said.

"Is that what you think?"

"Now don't go getting all defensive about it, my dear man. I do believe our little blond river rat has the right idea." She smiled at him, flirting, as they started along the dirt road into Bell Ridge.

"Jemima Longborn would make a good story."

"Not. my style." Chutney laughed, shaking her head. "That lady doesn't need any help. She can take care of herself."

They walked down the dark street in silence. One of the local saloons, the Golden Horseshoe, was beginning to perk up in the early evening. Loud voices and clinking glass drifted out into the cold night.

"Will you tell me where we're going?" Chutney asked.

"Sure."

"Well?"

"Here." The sign hanging out over the street showed a black horse painted on a white background.

"A stable. You cowboys plan some wild nights."

"Evening," Cord said to the proprietor as they entered

the barn. The proprietor was a thin, pale man with the red welt of a recent horseshoe print on his cheekbone. "I need a carriage for a few hours."

"Only one in town," the proprietor said as he led them to a dusty black carriage tucked in a lonely corner of the livery stable. The single wide seat was done in black leather, and it was soft to the touch. "Not much use for a fancy rig like this in Bell Ridge. Once in a while I take the missus out for a ride."

"Sounds like a good idea," Cord said.

"That'll be three dollars, with the roan."

Cord frowned. The stableman was asking at least double what he should be getting. "Two dollars," Cord said. His black eyes gripped and held those of the stableman, who swallowed once, deeply.

"Two dollars. I'll hitch her up." The man wiped away the hay dust on the seat before disappearing into the shadows for the roan. In a few minutes the rig was ready to go.

"The lady would like something to keep her warm," Cord told the man.

"The lady would," Chutney agreed.

"One bearskin," said the stableman without hesitation, thinking of the extra six bits he was making on the deal. He passed Chutney the thick mound of fur, which she arranged around herself.

"That was the biggest griz in California at one time," the man said. "Still is, but he's dead. Ain't seen a griz skin bigger'n that, dead *or* alive."

"This remind you of anything you've fought lately, Mr. Diamondback?" Chutney asked.

"Some, but it's not as feisty," he replied. She laughed.

The iron-rimmed wheels of the carriage clattered along the rocky road into the hills. Chutney slipped part of the bearskin over Diamondback, and then a soft hand slid across his thigh and clasped firmly over the bulge of his crotch. He felt himself harden.

"How does a man like you decide the right place to stop the carriage?"

"I usually let the horse worry about it," he said, but he gently pulled back on the reins, slowing the roan to a walk. A quarter mile out of town was as good as ten miles, out here in the woods. Cord peered into the darkness, looking for a spot off the road. Not likely someone would be coming along, but no sense in inviting trouble.

There. A thin spot in the bushes presented itself in the starlight. Beyond were the huge dark shapes of cotton-wood trees. With a light flick of his wrists, Cord urged the animal forward.

"Small stream up ahead," he told her. "Listen." The water shushed quietly in the night, and above them stars filled the sky.

"You are a *wonder*, Mr. Diamondback."

The roan moved along cautiously in the darkness, watching her footing in the patchy dirt near the stream. Cord let her have her head. No rush.

Chutney pulled the thick bearskin more tightly around her and leaned against him. Cord felt a small breast rub lightly across his upper arm.

"What happens if there's a flash flood?" she murmured as she snuggled closer.

"Then I guess you'll have a headline story for your paper."

Chutney tugged herself up so that her arms were wrapped around his neck and she was staring into his face. "You think I don't know when to stop working?"

"I guess we'll soon find out." His arms went around

the slim body and he eased her mouth to his. Her mouth opened as he ran his tongue against her lips, but her own tongue darted into hiding.

She felt different from a western woman. He wondered what the difference was. Maybe it was the feel of her fashionable silk clothes—clothes most western women forsook in favor of outfits that would stand up to the dirt and dust of western towns—or her coyness. Despite the warmth of her kiss she seemed content to wait for him to lead. Western women demanded less ritual and more action.

She was different. Cord liked the difference.

The shallow stream bed branched up ahead, disappearing into two thin receiving lines of cottonwoods. The roan made its way into the creek for a drink. The carriage's thin wheels straddled the stream. Carefully, the roan splashed through the shallow water, working her way farther upstream.

"Whoa," Cord said quietly.

They sat, neither speaking. The night was quiet; even the summer insects were quiet. The Milky Way was a glowing band through the cottonwoods.

"Deluxe accommodations," Cord said.

"Not quite yet," Chutney countered. She pushed herself back across the black leather seat of the carriage, tucking her feet in behind Diamondback and stretching out along the seat. "C'mon, Judge, get in here," she said.

Cord rearranged the flap of bearskin and felt her shiver at the rush of cold air. Then he was under the cover and she was working at his belt with swift movements, unbuckling it, undoing the strip of buttons down his crotch with anxious hands.

"Take it easy," he said.

"Why?"

Without answering, he worked the buttons of her blouse. In a moment his big hand cupped a breast. He felt the nipple swell and rise as he slid it between his lips. He heard her suck in her breath sharply, and then she moaned. He peeled away her blouse as he ran his tongue over her breasts, so that she was naked to the waist, flat belly pressed against him.

She began to undo the buttons of his shirt. Gently he wrapped his fingers around her busy hands and stopped her from going on.

"What's the matter?" she panted.

"Leave the shirt on."

The golden eyes glinted. "I want to feel you against me. Get that shirt off." She redoubled her efforts to unbutton the shirt.

He pulled her hands away, firmly pulling them behind her, and gripped both her slim wrists in one big hand. Her arms strained against his strength. The small breasts rose on her chest as the muscles flared under her soft skin.

"Come on, buster, get that shirt off," she ordered.

Cord laughed and brought her close, feeling the nipples rise in greeting. Lifting her against him, his lips touched hers gently, then harder, as the fire rose within him. He could feel her anger, but her mouth opened and her searching tongue slid into his mouth.

"What's the matter, Judge, afraid to take off your shirt?" she panted.

This time he let her finish the job. Then their bodies were naked against each other as they huddled under the bearskin. His hardened penis stood between her closed thighs. She reached down and wrapped a soft hand around his shaft, caressing it against her thigh. "The power of the press," she murmured. He laughed and pulled her closer to kiss the warm, small mouth. Her small hands went around him; he felt them exploring the ridges of muscle along his back.

"I thought you knew when to quit working," he said. Quickly he reached behind him and drew her hands away as they were about to touch the thick lacing of scars down his back.

"What are you talking about?" Chutney spoke with injured innocence.

"Your hands are getting into high-priced territory."

"Well, it's not as if I'm carrying a camera."

"Are you positive?"

She laughed. "If I could, I would."

"I know."

The scars were one reason he had brought her into the country rather than making love in the electric-lamp brightness of the *Clancy Longborn*. Once a reporter, always a reporter; by the time she was done she'd have investigated every inch of him.

"Why did you drag me out here when we could just as easily have stayed aboard the *Clancy* where it was warm?" she asked. She nuzzled his ear with a wet tongue, nipping at the earlobe gently.

"Things are going to be rough back there before this trip is over. I didn't want to find us in the middle of it. You've got a good story there—you're missing a bet."

She shifted impatiently. "What are you talking about? Helen of the Sacramento back there? The face that launched a hundred steamboats?" She snorted. "The woman probably reeks of coal smoke and bear grease. About as romantic as a goat."

"Don't let jealousy get in the way of a good story."

Chutney pulled away from him angrily. "Don't tell me how to handle my job, *Judge*. If anybody knows where a story's hidden, I do."

"How about if it's right out there in the open?"

"I'm the best damn reporter either side of the Mississippi," she cried. "And I know it!"

"The loudest anyway," he retorted.

"You're impossible!" she said, this time in a fierce whisper. "Why are you trying to ruin a perfectly delightful evening?"

He whistled softly and nodded. "Lost my head."

"Difficult enough to make love under a *griz* in the middle of winter, without you making trouble," she complained.

"Shut up."

Her hand burrowed down between their naked bodies, searching for his penis. "Can't argue and stay hard at the same time, huh, Judge," she taunted.

"Depends on the company."

She shut up then and returned his kiss, hard, as if she were trying to push her mouth through his own. As if the hardness of the kiss were a measure of its success.

"Relax, will you?"

He held her to him lightly and soon her tensed muscles relaxed. He slid a finger into her. She was waiting for him, wet and slippery already.

She hissed in delight. Then she was on her knees, her lips nibbling at the tip of his penis and her tongue rapidly flicking. Her hands went around his buttocks as she pulled his hips to her. He felt his penis enter her throat, deeper and deeper, until the entire length disappeared in her and her lips pressed softly against the very base of his pulsing organ, squeezing lightly so that his balls rose and fell slightly in a tiny ebb and flow. Slowly, she pulled back on the shaft and Cord could feel the walls of her throat sliding along the swelled ridges of his veined penis. She was humming quietly. He could feel the vibration without hearing it, feel the echo deep in his balls. The vibrations died away as she slid her mouth away.

Panting, she pulled herself up slowly. She climbed his muscled chest. Her hands massaged the muscled ridges of his chest, rhythmically caressing his sides, carefully working around toward the path of scars that studded his spine. She hoisted herself onto him, her wet vagina sliding onto his hardness.

"Goin' somewhere?"

"I'm there," she moaned throatily. "Oh, God, I'm there."

Despite her evident pleasure in riding him, she was searching for the scars. He wasn't worried. Finding them would be one more bit of information for her sharp little mind to mull over, but nothing conclusive. Her feeling the web of scar tissue wouldn't convict him any more than he already had been. If she decided to write about it, he'd only be so much column fodder in her newspaper.

Suddenly, before she even neared his spinal cord, her nails were digging deep into his sides, tearing furrows as she peaked in ecstasy. Under the heavy bearskin her teeth sank into the flesh above his collarbone, and he could hear the stifled scream of passion. She rose and dropped on his penis like a piledriver, thudding onto him so that the carriage springs squeaked steadily and the roan looked around.

Chutney's face lifted away from his chest a half inch.

"So good, so good," she whispered, more to herself than to Cord.

His strong hands lifted and turned her so that she was kneeling on all fours on the floor of the carriage. He rearranged the bearskin so that they were covered as he reared behind her. His penis seemed to gain in weight as it slid over the cleft of her buttocks and she moaned again, the warm mist of her breath fogging the night air.

Then he entered her vagina, the thick shaft sliding home, touching bottom deep inside her as she let out an animal growl of pleasure. She squeezed her legs together, and the dark tunnel of her gripped his organ along its length.

"Ohhhh, Cord . . ." She tried to rock forward, but his big hands gripped her hips hard, stopping her. Then he slid her forward slowly, teasing, contracting his muscles so that the head of his penis bobbed inside her.

Suddenly he slammed her backward toward him, his shaft sinking deep into her, and she yelped in pleasure.

"Oh, yes, oh, yes," she mumbled in a trance of ecstasy.

Then he was thrusting into her, long, deep strokes that built the pressure in him like a piston. She reached back between her legs and cupped his balls in her hand, and he detonated with a deep-throated cry that echoed away into the still night.

Fiercely, he pushed himself into her. She urged him deeper, wedging her free arm into the corner of the carriage, bracing herself to help him enter her further. "More, more, more," she chanted.

His uncontrollable urgency propelled him onward. He gripped her shoulders and held her tightly to him.

Then she was in his arms, pulling herself up to him, her fingers working their way carefully up the braid of scars along his spine as if they were climbing a ladder. The grizzly skin slipped away and they were naked to the cold night. Let it go, Cord thought. He felt relaxed, and the chill hadn't hit yet.

She raised her lips to his, pressing softly against them. "Wonderful. That . . . was . . . so . . . wonderful . . . Mister . . . Deacon."

A blinding flash of whiteness suddenly flooded the carriage with daylight. A muted boom rolled over Cord as he tried to twist himself around. And as he pulled away from Chutney Crane, he heard the double click of a revolver. Very close to the side of his head.

# 14

Even as the second click of the revolver's hammer was echoing into the night, Cord was driving his right forearm upward. Bare flesh punched the cold metal gun barrel toward the stars. More blinding white light exploded only inches from Cord's eyes. The revolver's bellow ripped through his skull.

"Shit!" Cord heard. He dived toward the sound. A vague black shape still hidden in the afterimage of the burning gunpowder was trying to aim at him again. Chutney's cry of pain reached him as she was battered against the carriage frame by the force of Cord's exit.

His bare feet hit the muddy water below, and Cord flung himself at the shape. The gun fired again and he felt a shock wave riffle his hair as the bullet screamed past his ear. The roan whinnied in fear and began dragging the carriage forward in the stream. There was a crash of metal and breaking glass that pricked at his memory, but he couldn't take the time to identify it.

Cord slammed a shoulder into the muscled body, driving it backward until it tripped and smacked into the freezing stream. The revolver splashed out of reach. Three quick rights only enraged the man beneath him.

"You son of a bitch!" the man growled, and caught Cord on the side of the head with the back of a big fist.

Clay Gibbs.

With the punch, Cord rolled away, his naked body skidding across the ankle-deep water as he struggled for footing. Jagged stones bit into his feet. Unbalanced again, he dropped to his knees.

"Clay! My God, what are you doing?" Chutney shouted from the carriage.

Gibbs came at Cord silently, crouching, and Cord realized the photographer had a knife. Clothed and armed, Gibbs had the advantage. Cord felt his muscles tightening from the cold. In a few more seconds he wouldn't have the flexibility to defend himself and the Easterner would be able to sink the knife deep into his bare belly.

"Ahhh!" A sharp, fist-sized stone tumbled under Cord's foot as he stepped on it in the darkness. Quickly, he reached down and plucked it up. A weapon.

Gibbs lunged at him with a snarl, coming straight in, looking for the quick kill. Cord backpedaled out of the stream, sucked in, and the blade slashed air, barely missing him.

He had no chance to use the rock in his hand as he staggered backward, tripping against the stream embankment hidden by the darkness. He scrambled up the short, grassy slope. Gibbs was a dark mass slashing sidearm at him. Cord felt the knife slice against his shinbone and hot pain erupted. Gibbs's boots slipped on the grassy embankment and he bent over, fingers to the ground, regaining his balance.

Cord saw his chance. As Gibbs straightened and charged up the embankment, Cord's right arm rocketed through its arc. The stone crashed into the Easterner's shoulder with the dull whump of a hard punch, stopping him in his tracks.

With a step, Cord launched himself into the night air, both feet leading the way to the dark shadow that was Clay Gibbs's unprotected jaw. Cord's heels snapped outward, and with a scream Gibbs fell to the ground.

Cord drove in with his heel again, this time just below Gibbs's solar plexus, and the Easterner balled himself up in pain. Did he still have the knife?

Cord quickly reached down and grabbed the man's right arm, twisting it upward. The knife flicked and disappeared into the grass on the embankment.

"Noooo!" Gibbs was a writhing mass of agony. Cord yanked him to his feet and drove a fist into his stomach again and again until Gibbs sagged forward breathlessly.

"Cord! Are you all right?" Chutney's frightened voice called from the carriage. The roan had wedged the rig between two cottonwoods. "Cord, what's going on?"

Gibbs lay crumpled helplessly in the stream, gasping for breath. He wasn't going anywhere under his own power for a while. Cord headed for the carriage.

"Give me my clothes." Quickly he pulled himself into the carriage and slid his denims over his hips. He was freezing. He pulled on his shirt and coat.

"Is he all right?" Chutney was dressed, but she was also shivering, trying to pull the huge bearskin tighter around her.

"Was this some scheme of yours?" he demanded coldly.

"No, Cord, I swear it! He's acting like a crazy man!"

"Why didn't you tell me he took such a proprietary interest in you?" Cord tugged on one boot, then the other.

"He doesn't own me. But sometimes he thinks he does."

"He sure acts like it." Cord remembered something. The first flash of light. It hadn't been a gunshot. And the sound of breaking glass.

He jumped out of the carriage and moved behind it. The

crushed hulk of another of Gibbs's cameras lay in the stream, its holder for the magnesium flash illumination twisted and crumpled. Cord plucked it out of the water. Walking back to the carriage, he flung the camera remains onto the floor next to Chutney.

"How do you like posing for your buddy's pictures? Is it worth it for a story?"

"I didn't know, Cord," Chutney pleaded quietly.

Quickly Cord unsnapped one of the reins from the roan's bridle. Then he made his way back to Gibbs.

"Smile for the camera—Cord Diamondback!" Gibbs hissed triumphantly, although he was still lying on the muddy edge of the stream. He began to laugh, but his laughter quickly broke down into short gasps of pain.

"Shut up," Cord said.

"What's it worth to you for me to shut up? Five thousand dollars? That's what it's going to take." Again Gibbs laughed weakly. "Five thousand for a picture of a scarred back."

"You don't have a picture, Gibbs."

"Why not?"

"Seems as if your camera suffered a little accident."

"You bastard," Gibbs gritted. "It doesn't matter, though. No five thousand dollars, and I tell everybody what I saw. They'll lynch you on the spot."

"All you saw was something no newspaper will print. Not even the *Daily Intelligencer*."

"I swear I'll spread it around if I don't get that money, Diamondback, or Deacon, or whatever your name is. When Chutney gets it from New York, you give it to me."

"Why? Your paper is paying for pictures of my back. And for five thousand dollars you can take all you want. What happens when Chutney gives away the five thousand dollars and comes back with no pictures?"

"You don't plan to show your back, even if you get the money," Gibbs accused.

"Why not?"

"Because the scars prove you're Christopher Deacon."

"The scars only prove that I found an easy way of making five thousand dollars. I'm more than happy to let you take the pictures—but not before I collect the money."

Gibbs was quiet for a moment. He wasn't sure if Cord was bluffing.

"How'd you find us?" Cord said.

"I followed you when you left the boat. Thank you for not goin' any further out of town. I was gettin' real tired of lugging that camera." Gibbs tried to roll over, but he groaned with the pain in his injured arm.

"If I had wanted a foursome, I'd have invited you and your camera along."

"Nobody messes with my woman and gets away with it. I'll get you one way or another, Diamondback!" Gibbs threatened.

Cord pulled Gibbs upward by the front of his coat and drove his fist into his jaw. Gibbs slumped back to the mud. Cord began cinching Gibbs's arms tightly with the leather rein. "Not tonight, you won't."

"What are you going to do with him?" Chutney asked.

"He earned himself a long stay in my cabin closet."

"But, but, he'll be useless to me!" Chutney sputtered. "I need him to take pictures."

"You should have kept your boyfriend on a shorter leash, then."

Chutney looked uncomfortable.

"Well, somehow he's got the impression that I'm messing with *his* woman. How do you suppose he got that?"

"We get along okay. And he'll shoot any picture I want

him to. I never told him there was anything serious between us, though."

"When he tries to kill me, it's serious," Cord said.

"Look, I can handle him," Chutney said. "I'll make sure he doesn't give you any more trouble."

"He's already planning to keep the five thousand for himself."

"What?"

"Sounds as if he's not pleased with you," Cord told her. "He wants to get even with both of us."

"Oh, Clay is all big talk," Chutney said with a dismissing wave of her hand. "I can wrap him around my little finger."

"I don't intend to get myself killed."

"I'd say that's a distinct possibility, no matter what you intend. And not just because of Clay."

Cord dragged the unconscious body to the carriage. He hoisted Gibbs onto the platform behind the carriage seat.

"I'll cool him off when we get back to the boat," Chutney said.

Cord didn't reply.

"Look, the race tonight will take his mind off this. Give him a camera and something dramatic to shoot and he becomes obsessed. Remember, you demolished one of his cameras—two of them, now. Do you understand how photographers feel about their cameras? His natural instinct was to blow your head off. You really ought to think more carefully about the long term before you get into fights with people, Cord."

"Tomorrow is long term."

"Anyway," she said, rustling around under the bearskin, "the race has interesting possibilities as a story. You've finally hooked me, Mr. Cord Diamondback Deacon. I'm suddenly as interested in how we will live through this night in a riverboat race as I am in seeing what your charming back looks like in the light of day.''

Cord guided the roan back to the dirt road to Bell Ridge.

''Do you know anything about syphilis?'' he asked.

''What?''

''Do you know anything about syphilis?''

''Wait a minute,'' Chutney said, alarmed. ''You're not going to tell me that you—''

''Have syphilis? No. But J. K. Barber does.''

''So what?''

''It's in the final stages. He's completely unpredictable. Capable of anything in that race tonight.''

''What are you driving at?''

''Very simple. This is Barber's only chance to keep the *Westerner* afloat. If both boats stay on the river, there won't be enough traffic to support them. The railroad will eat them up, no matter how many friends Barber has. And he knows that.''

''Do you think that's going to make him even more squirrelly?'' Chutney asked.

''Maybe.''

''What do you think he'll do? He can't very well ram us again. We'll be going in the same direction.''

''Unfortunately, there's more than one way to sink a riverboat.''

# 15

"Well? Will you let me have him?" Chutney said.

Gibbs lay still on the back of the carriage, his face pressed against the back of the seat, his mouth open like a bass going for a fat worm.

"Long as you keep him away from me," Cord replied. "He *scares* me."

"After you beat him silly, he scares you?"

Cord's dark eyes glinted in the light from the *Clancy*. "I'm as peaceable a person as you'd want to meet. I don't enjoy fights."

"You're a curious mixture, all right," Chutney agreed. "Tough one moment, modest the next. You certainly can be most pleasant when you want to be."

Cord nodded coolly and got out of the carriage. He circled past Gibbs's unconscious body and offered his hand to Chutney.

"And make sure *I* get the five thousand."

"I'll straighten it out," Chutney promised. She made sure she stood close to him, Cord noted, as she spoke quietly so he could feel her warm breath running up his neck and over his ear.

He went to the back of the carriage and began unlashing

Gibbs's inert form. A couple of sharp taps on the cheek brought the photographer around. He groaned and his eyes opened.

"Come on, Clay, fun's over," Chutney said. "Let's see if you can act like a big boy for a change."

They got him upright. Still wobbly, he rested himself against Chutney. "Okay, big fella?" she asked, as if she had nursed him through these beatings before. When he was able to stand, she led him toward the landing stage.

"Thank you for a very nice evening," she said, half turning back to Cord. "I'm sorry we weren't able to get the interview."

"I'm not."

"Well, there's tomorrow, Cord. And I'll be expecting a truly elegant judging job on the race tonight." She clicked up the landing plank in her fashionable boots, Gibbs in tow.

Cord returned the carriage to the livery stable and walked back to the *Clancy*. Ten P.M. No sense trying to sleep now, even though he had an hour before the meeting with Jemima and J. K. Barber. The bruises Bobo had inflicted the night before were still hurting, particularly after his bout with Clay Gibbs.

Certainly, Chutney was an attractive woman, he reflected. Too confident in that respect. She relied on her beauty to melt the men with whom she came into contact. Wasn't quite sure how to deal with the situation if a man didn't lunge for her like a grizzly after a colt.

He made his way up to the saloon. Might as well have a beer before looking up Jemima.

The *Clancy*'s main saloon at night bore little resemblance to the dark, almost church-quiet place he'd been in the day before. In the mirrors, the chandeliers seemed to multiply into a forest of blazing crystal trees. An upright piano thumped away in the far corner, near the broad staircase leading to the lower deck. Cigar smoke was thick against the high ceiling, thinning slightly at table level where gamblers in black wool frockcoats were sizing up their rivals.

Most of the saloon crowd were men, three or four hundred of them, Cord estimated, but women moved among them like gold carp among the stones in a riverbed. The dancing girls each wore a single black floppy feather rising from a bun at the back of each of their heads, and bright red rouge and red lipstick marked them from the wives aboard.

Jemima Longborn stood alongside the swinging doors, watching the noisy scene like the mistress of a boarding school. Despite the evening finery of her employees and paying customers, she wore her usual work pants and scorched leather jacket.

"Good business here," Cord remarked.

"Not bad, if I can keep the girls from getting a little side work from the customers. No whoring on the *Clancy*, as far as I'm concerned," Jemima said. "My daddy didn't allow it, either. Once he took two of those ladies that he caught coming out of the passengers' rooms, tucked one under each arm, and tossed them overboard as we went past Lime Shallows pier. Word got around." She paused. "My daddy sure was funny that way, because as soon as he made shore he'd shag himself up to Beulah's in San Francisco, or Cora Mae Elliot's place in Sacramento, and I wouldn't see him for two days. Nothing aboard the boat, though. He said he always liked it better when the ride was done. Said it put a good cuttin' edge on his orneriness, he called it. And you wonder why they think my daddy is peculiar."

"Not your average steamboat captain," Cord agreed.

Jemima looked him over, noting his wet pants and boots. "Guess you've had your rest and refreshment for the evening," she said. "What are you doing up here?"

Was he mistaken, or did she sound angry?

"Thought we'd do a little planning before we met with Barber."

Without warning, an oak chair flew through the smoky air, crashing through the beer mugs and whiskey glasses atop a nearby table and smashing it. Women screamed. Like a puff of dust squirting from a dirty rug, people scattered from the fight that had suddenly blossomed in the back corner of the saloon.

"Hey!" Jemima yelled, and moved toward the fight. Cord circled to the left.

"You want to push somebody around, mister, go out and find yourself a heifer that fits. You keep your shit-smelling face out of decent company, you got it?" It was Arthur Tellock. And he was holding a derringer, a .41-caliber Remington, on Cheat Grimes. The derringer would kill at fifty feet. At ten feet, Grimes wouldn't have a chance.

"I'm gonna rip you up the middle," Grimes swore. "That little tickler ain't gonna help you worth a damn," he said, but he made no move to go for the gambler.

"Come on, break it up," Jemima ordered, stepping between the two men. Grimes, I'm charging you for everything busted in here, and if you bust any more, I'll go get the marshal."

"This fool—"

"I don't care who did what," Jemima said wearily. "Grimes, get your butt off this boat or you're gonna wind up in jail."

Despite Jemima's threat to Grimes, Arthur Tellock's spectacles were overheating with his anger and exasperation.

They began to steam over with the swampy heat of the saloon.

"Cool down, Tellock," Cord cautioned. "Won't do you any good to kill him."

Suddenly Diamondback was thrown off his feet as if he had been standing inside a kettledrum that someone had just whammed with all his might. The wild concussion was followed by a roaring explosion that seemed to lift the starboard side of the *Clancy* and drop it back on the river. Tinkling crazily, the electric chandeliers flickered and went out. In the darkness and panic, flames could be seen rising from the river side of the steamboat, blindingly bright against the darkness.

Men were shouting, women screaming as the first sharp bite of smoke dug into their unprotected lungs.

"Fire! Fire!" The panicked screams only served to madden the already confused crowd in the saloon. The mirrors on the bulkheads had shattered with the force of the explosion, sending spatters of broken glass into the frightened passengers.

"Jemima! Get to the fire! I'll clear the saloon!" Cord yelled to the woman. In the ghastly glow of the firelight, Jemima nodded and began to fight her way through the mob. She worked toward the bar, in the direction of the flames that were licking up the starboard bulkhead of the *Clancy Longborn*. Cord could see the filigree that adorned the superstructure already being devoured by the flames, and the burning paint was searing his lungs.

Jemima vaulted to the top of the bar, danced over the maddened drunks trying to use it as a highway to escape, and headed for the packed door.

Cord was preoccupied with the frightened people trying to force themselves from the smoky saloon. A wave of them had spilled down the staircase to the lower deck, but others were vaulting the rail and dropping onto the heads below. The wide staircase was crammed with people unable to worm their way to safety.

"We're gonna die! We're gonna die!" one madman screamed, his eyes wide and white as he stood frozen against the far bulkhead.

A big miner in blue suspenders and red flannel shirt had broken a leg off an oak bar stool and was flailing the unprotected backs of people trying to escape. Cord's eyes were running tears with the thick, resinous smoke that was filling the saloon.

"Hey! Save your energy," Cord said to the miner, spinning him around to get his attention.

The miner had the trapped, panicky stare that Cord had seen on men who had been caught in mines hundreds of feet below ground with no way to escape. Rescued, they'd stay in the open for days rather than risk the crushing closeness of even a large room.

The miner's mouth opened soundlessly and he brought the stool leg back with both hands as if it were a billy club.

Cord delivered a left deep into the miner's sagging belly. The bar-stool leg thunked to the floor as the miner dropped to his knees and hugged his stomach.

"Calm down, dammit!" Cord shouted. "Look! It's mostly smoke! You're not going to die!" It was true. Cord saw that the flames weren't riddling the entire boat. Around him, people were beginning to regain their senses. Cord soon found himself outside in the chilly night.

Flames caressed the river side of the *Clancy*. Amid the smoke it was impossible for Cord to see what actual damage was being done. The boat wasn't listing. The hull must still be intact.

"Let's go! Get down there and help. Let's get those

buckets moving!" he shouted to a group of men who seemed to be milling around purposelessly. "What's the matter?"

A man on the lower deck with a red bandanna over his face to ward off the smoke silently held something up toward Diamondback. In the light of the flames, Cord could see a piece of skull with a hank of hair still attached. The hair was wet—wet with water, not blood.

"Looks as if somebody tried to blow up the *Clancy* and blew himself up instead," the man shouted over the crackling fire.

The flames licked up the thin wood curlicues that decorated the outboard side of the *Clancy*. "Water! Water! Water!" came the rhythmic cries as volunteers on both sides of the flames doused the fire with buckets of river water. The defense was working. Bit by bit the men were beating back the flames.

Cord scanned the crowd as he passed buckets up the line, his muscular forearms swelling with the steady pump of bucket after endless bucket.

Then he spotted Cheat Grimes. Barber's henchman was looking down from the saloon deck, calmly watching the firefighters. Then he lit a stump of cigar, casually flicking the burning match toward the volunteers. It was just another burning piece of ash among the glowing bits that floated into the air on the rising streams of heat from the fire. No one but Diamondback noticed the contemptuous movement. Grimes strode away, disappearing into the haze of smoke that enveloped the boat.

It was almost as if Grimes had expected the fire to occur. The timing of the fight with Arthur Tellock; it could have been planned to bring Jemima running, distract anyone who might see a swimmer approaching the side of the

*Clancy* with enough dynamite to turn the *Clancy* into a useless pile of splintered wood.

The danger dwindled. Quickly, the flames retreated before the bucket brigades. Cheers erupted from the onlookers, and the volunteers began feeling proud of themselves.

"Not much damage," someone said. "Just scorched, mostly. Dumb bastard blowed hisself up and barely scratched the *Clancy*. Old Clancy himself woulda been proud."

Men's voices muttered satisfied agreement.

Cord abandoned the bucket brigade. Quickly he moved across the deck in time to see Cheat Grimes walking up the landing stage. Cord followed.

# 16

Cheat Grimes strode quickly down the same alley he had taken earlier to reach the boat yard. Cord could just make him out, a shadow among the shadows of the silent buildings. Then he heard the hasp freed on a door and Grimes disappeared into one of the anonymous barns that backed up to the Bell Ridge wharf.

Cord quietly worked his way forward. It was dead silent. The alley probably didn't see too much legitimate business this time of night. The only noise drifted over from the *Clancy*, where the piano had started up again. Anybody up at this time of night was at the steamboat, speculating about the exact nature of the explosion and fire.

The loose-fitting boards of the barn Grimes had entered let the light of an oil lamp filter through. Apparently there was a back office in the barn.

Cord slipped down the narrow gap between the buildings to where the light shone through the cracks. Wood scraps littered the passageway, forcing him to feel his way carefully. A loosened block of pine rattled through the pile and he froze, but the buzz of the voices continued.

The weathered boards overlapped. Cord couldn't make

out any of the people inside, and the voices were
muffled.

One way in. The front door.

Breathing shallowly, he edged back to the alley. The
hasp on the barn door freed itself of its crosspiece when he
lifted it and made no noise as he slipped it off the staple.

The front part of the barn was used to store hay. It was
about half full, the hay bales piled in random stacks.
Pulling the door shut, he planted each foot carefully as he
moved over the dirt floor, shifting his weight smoothly to
avoid making a sound. Lessons learned in his cavalry days
flooded back. Noiselessly, he pressed himself into a crev-
ice in the bales of hay five feet from the office door, but
out of direct line of sight, even if they came out.

"Somebody fished a piece of scalp out of the river," he
heard Cheat Grimes say. "Must'a been Burly's."

"Goddamn Burly." It was J. K. Barber's nasal voice.
The short, chopped sentences marked him. The syphilis
was destroying him. "Lit the dynamite too soon. Hadn't
reached the boat. Chickenshit."

"What do we do now?" Grimes asked.

"We race. What the hell you think?" Barber took a
deep, rattling breath. "I want Longborn off the river.
Once and for all. Nothing says we have to roll over. Play
dead."

"I thought the *Clancy* is faster than the *Westerner*,"
Grimes said.

"Old man Longborn said so. Doesn't matter. She draws
even with us, we finish her."

"You're playing too rough, J. K." The voice sounded
like that of the boat-yard owner. "You're acting crazier
every day. People are starting to complain. Pretty soon the
boys in San Francisco aren't going to be able to cover for
you."

"Hell with 'em. I cover myself."

There was silence for a moment.

"You've still got two immediate problems," the boat-yard owner pointed out. "The marshal. And the judge."

"The judge." Barber sneered. "Diamondback is good cover. We can say we tried to settle peaceably. Thought he'd be honest. Can't help it if he tried to cheat us. Can kill him if we need to."

A whiff of cigar smoke reached Cord when Barber paused.

"Ignore the marshal," Barber continued, panting with the exertion of talking. "Brake won't stop us from leaving. Two-bit town here. Can't afford to lose any river business. He threatens, I threaten back. We work out of Lime Shallows. Let the good people of Bell Ridge know their marshal drove our business away."

"The Central Pacific owns Brake," countered the boat-yard owner. "He may be looking for an excuse to jump you. I hear he's planning to be senator."

"Can we buy a pass?"

"Maybe. Maybe not. Brake's unpredictable. Likes to throw his weight around. And he's already got his jaw unhinged about your collision this morning."

"Then he will be real happy about the explosion on the *Clancy*." Barber wheezed a laugh. "Might stop her."

"Hard to tell, J. K. If Brake has as much pull with the railroad as they say, he could squeeze you. Hard."

"Not for long."

Another silence. "What does that mean? That you'd kill him?" Another silence. "You're out of control, J. K.," the boat-yard owner said uneasily. "You're pushing all this too far. They hear we've been talking about killing a marshal and they'll stretch our necks sure as pee is yellow."

"What time is it?" Barber demanded.

Cord heard the clink of a watch chain. "Eleven-fifteen." He moved deeper into the shadows.

"You'd better get back there or it's gonna look a little bit funny that you're missing while the *Clancy* burns," the boat-yard man warned.

"One more thing," Barber said. "What I need from you is—"

To Cord's left the barn door let out a loud screech as the hasp dragged over the staple. Barber stopped abruptly as the door swung open a foot. Cord heard rapid footsteps running down the alley.

"Son of a bitch!" Barber snapped. Then Cheat Grimes was slamming out the barn door in pursuit of the intruder. Cord edged himself into the dark corner of the hay bales, touching the holster at his hip to see that the Smith & Wesson .45 was in place.

A woman's cry was cut short in the alley and Cord could hear the muffled sounds of a struggle. Barber and the boat-yard owner had followed Grimes as far as the door.

The door opened wider. In the dim lamplight from the office, Cord saw that Grimes had captured Chutney Crane. The longshoreman had a massive hand clamped over the reporter's mouth and her right arm was bent up behind her back. Tears glistened in the lamplight. Chutney's booted foot tried to kick back at Grimes's shin, but he tugged her arm back a little more and Cord heard her stifled groan of pain.

"C'mon, bitch," Grimes spat.

Grimes shoved her toward the office, with Barber close behind and angry. He flung his cigar to the dirt and ground it in. The boat-yard man pulled the door shut.

"Anybody else out there?"

"Nah," Grimes said. "She was alone. Snoopin'."

"Who is she?" Barber demanded.

"Some nosy reporter from back East. Saw her hangin' around with Diamondback earlier."

"What are you doing here?" Barber said to Chutney. "You're over your head here, lady."

"Not quite," Chutney said scornfully.

"What you up to?"

"Seein' as how it was your men who tried to finish off the *Clancy,* I'd say you are number-one story in Bell Ridge at the moment. Not to mention a lot of other places."

"You're off base, lady. We had nothing to do with it."

"We'll see."

"Smart. Too smart." Barber must have turned to Grimes. "How'd she figure to come here?"

"I dunno, boss," Cheat Grimes whined. "There was nobody behind me. I looked."

"You can't let her go now," the boat-yard owner said.

"Okay," Barber said decisively. "Get her to the boat."

"If I disappear, every newspaper on the East Coast will come digging around to find out what happened," Chutney threatened.

Barber laughed. "They'll be after Jemima. Not me."

"What are you going to do?" Chutney demanded.

"Get her out of here," Barber said, ignoring her. "Keep her quiet."

"Leave me alo—" Chutney's voice was cut off.

Cord waited in the darkness. He could rescue her now, but it wouldn't solve anything. Barber would only be off the river temporarily, thanks to his powerful friends. And Chutney might appreciate the rescue, but not enough to sit on a story about him. No, there was a better way.

"Tie her up," Barber said. "Don't let anyone see her."

"How will we get her in, boss?" Cheat Grimes asked.

"Hell. Put her under coal. Or wood. Hoist her onto the

deck. Stick her in my cabin. I've got to meet with Longborn and the judge.''

Barber lurched through the semidarkness in front of Diamondback. He turned back toward the doorway where Cord could hear Grimes working on Chutney Crane.

"Tell Boils to get the engine going," Barber ordered. "And be ready to leave. Fast."

# 17

"Let's get this over with," Barber said. "Race to Sandy Bar. First one through wins. The other boat gets off the river. Forever. Right?"

"As long as both boats get *on* the river," Cord amended.

The ivory toothpick dancing around near the left jowl of Barber's mouth stopped momentarily as Barber studied Cord suspiciously. "What's that supposed to mean?" he demanded. The syphilis-damaged nose was a black clump in the half-light of the docks.

"Okay, okay, let's wrap this up," Jemima said impatiently, not really hearing Cord's comment.

The *Westerner*'s winch hoisted a small load of wood toward the pilot deck. Chutney Crane would be there, bound and gagged. Cord idly wondered if she had ever gone to such lengths for a story.

"One last thing," he said, glancing from Jemima to Barber. "Five hundred dollars apiece, up front. For the judging. I get the rest when we land."

"Get my share from her," Barber said, turning away with a lurch. "I figure she's paying you enough for the decision."

"You're both buying my judging skills. Not my decision," Cord said.

Barber stopped and looked back at him. "Yeah. Right." He sneered.

Jemima peeled off five bills from the wad that appeared in her hand. "Guess I've got five hundred dollars' worth of advantage on the decision, right, Diamondback?"

"Won't help much if you don't beat him."

Fog was setting in again. The *Westerner's* single stack gave a preliminary burp as they stood in the darkness of the Bell Ridge wharf with the mist creeping around them. Cord thought of the *Clancy's* electrical lights, which had been damaged in the explosion. The big spotlight on the bow that would have illuminated the river ahead was out. Now Jemima would have to rely on the old oil-lamp reflector for night visibility. Not an encouraging thought, especially in the fog.

And she was being naive, not noticing the *Westerner's* hot stack. The *Clancy's* engine was silent, the boilers probably still cold. She actually expected Barber to wait for her to get an equal start.

Barber staggered back toward them, his pumpkin face suddenly splitting into a leering grin. "It'll be your last ride on the *Clancy,* sweetheart. Better enjoy it."

Before Cord could catch her arm, Jemima's bantam right fist came out of the darkness and caught Barber alongside the toothpick, momentarily squeezing and twisting the man's fat cheek. Almost before Barber's skin settled back into place, Jemima followed with another right. Barber reached over with surprising quickness and grabbed her wrist.

"Damn you, bitch," he snarled, and started to wrench her around as she fought wildly to free herself.

Diamondback's boot caught Barber on his elbow, kicking upward against the locked joint. Barber grunted in pain.

"You bastard." Barber reached for Diamondback.

"Dammit, let's quit jackin' around," Cord growled. "If you want to settle this, do it on the river." He looked from Barber to Jemima. "The rules are set. Let's get with it."

As he spoke, Cord noticed the marshal hurrying toward them through the fog. Barber also caught sight of Brake. He spun and began jogging toward the *Westerner*, raising his thumb in a signal. The *Westerner*'s stack was pumping smoke into the night and deck hands started casting off the lines.

"C'mon, Jemima, he's not going to wait for you. Get your ass moving!" Cord said sharply.

"Barber! Longborn! Hold up!" Brake yelled.

Jemima looked once at Diamondback and began sprinting for the *Clancy*. "Hoodoo! Get her going!"

Brake was puffing as he reached Cord. "You sure as hell better stop them, Diamondback," he panted, whipping his bearded face back and forth from one boat to the other like a hunting dog trying to decide between two dropped ducks.

"Why?" Cord said.

"Because if you don't, I'm going to arrest you on charges of conspiracy. And if those boats race tonight, I'll hit you with that too. I'll have all three of you before a grand jury." Barber's lips pulled back smugly over his yellowed teeth.

"Seems as if I don't have much to do with it," Cord observed.

"You won't when I lock you up tonight," Brake agreed, looking about wildly, still confused about where to start.

The *Westerner* chugged away from the wharf, her port paddle beating the river to a white froth as she accelerated.

The *Clancy*'s deck hands were untying her as her boilers fought for power.

"Sorry to interrupt, Marshal. I've got a boat to catch." Cord tipped his hat and suddenly broke for the *Clancy*.

"Hold up, Diamondback, or I'll shoot!" Brake yelled. Cord dug harder, flinging himself across the widening gap between the dock and the boat's stern. The *Clancy* inched forward, struggling to pick up speed.

Brake's Colt .45 barked twice in the fog, chipping slivers of wood from the *Clancy*'s bulkhead. Cord dived for the protected doorway as more shots erupted, the bullets singing through the oak panels around him.

"I'll get you, Diamondback! I'll get all of you!" Brake yelled. Then the staccato beat of the *Clancy*'s engines overwhelmed everything else as the boat clawed its way after its rival.

# 18

"Come on, Ty, get her goin'!" Jemima urged impatiently, shouting into the speaking tube. "What are you waitin' for?"

She put her ear to the tube.

"I said, get it goin'!" she shouted into the tube again, louder this time. Her fist rapped hard in frustration against the huge rosewood wheel that steered the *Clancy*.

"She's still gatherin' speed, Jemima. She's got more in her," cautioned Hoodoo. "Take it *easy*. I'll get you some coffee, 'fore you bust yer walkin' beam."

"C'mon, the son of a bitch is pullin' away," Jemima yelled into the night.

The *Westerner* was already a quarter mile ahead.

"We can't afford to give away this much," Jemima said worriedly. "I can probably get him by a horsehair on speed, but I don't know if I can catch him fast enough. Sandy Bar is to starboard. If I ain't a full length ahead of him at Sandy Bar, he'll squeeze me right into it."

"Any room up his port side?" Cord asked.

"Nàh. He made sure of that. Too shallow, even for the *Clancy*. We'd just be diggin' a trench."

"They've got Chutney Crane aboard," Cord said.

"What?"

"They kidnapped her. They're going to blame her death on you. They don't intend for you to make it through Sandy Bar, one way or another. In fact, you weren't even supposed to make it onto the river tonight. Brake messed up their plans."

Jemima stared grimly ahead into the darkness at the lights aboard the *Westerner*. "You knew all this and didn't tell me?"

"If I could have beaten Barber back to the boat, I would have told you. By the time I got here, you were arguing with him."

"But what about the woman?" Jemima asked after a moment's thought. "How did they get her? Why *her*?"

"They caught her trying to overhear a little conversation they were having about our future. So Barber figured he could solve all his problems at once. Get rid of you, me, and Chutney Crane at the same time. And his friends in San Francisco and Sacramento can smooth things over. Chutney might let the story out, so they decided to get rid of her too. Darkness. No witnesses."

Hoodoo came up and planted Jemima's mug of coffee next to the compass. "You sure as hell better win this race," he told her.

Something in his tone caught her attention. "What's that supposed to mean?"

"That we got four barrels of oil aboard. 'N a hundred pounds of bacon. Lean. I checked."

"No."

Hoodoo shrugged elaborately and walked away. "Suit yerself."

The darkened wheelhouse was silent. Jemima kept the *Clancy* a hair to starboard of the white wake trailing from the *Westerner*. The other boat was almost hidden by the fog. Barber might even have put a little more distance between them, Cord guessed.

Hoodoo offered a full mug of coffee to Diamondback, but his attention was still directed at Jemima.

"We got thirty barrels of whiskey back there too."

"I said *no*!" Jemima flashed. "I ain't gonna blow us all to hell for a race!"

"Yer daddy'd roll over in his grave, he knew you were bein' so damn *caw*-tious," Hoodoo criticized, now making no pretense of offering suggestions to her. "Them boilers are made of good ol' American steel, the best there is. They *ain't* gonna blow unless you got the devil hisself in there with his pitchfork. I seen yer daddy dump a whole barrel of oil into each of them boilers to get more speed. Back when he beat the hell out of the *Chrysopolis*—"

"Okay, okay," Jemima gave in. "Tell Ty to go careful, though."

"That bacon will give it a little extra oomph," Hoodoo pressed. "Touch o' that grease in them boilers and the *Clancy*'d take off and *fly* to Sacramento. Damn—"

"What about the whiskey?" Jemima countered. "Why don't you want to toss in a barrel of whiskey? Burn *good*."

Hoodoo's eyes lowered to the deck. "Well, hell, I thought we'd save the whiskey till we got really *desperate*. No sense in wasting good whiskey till you really need to."

Jemima laughed. "Hoodoo, you are one drowned river rat. You tell Ty to stick with the oil for now."

"Okay, Jemima." The old man hurried onto the hurricane deck, intent on delivering his message.

Neither of them said anything. The black smoke pouring almost invisibly from the *Westerner* wafted through the *Clancy*'s pilothouse.

Cord sniffed. "Barber's burning some oil already," he said.

"Barber would burn his grandmother if she'd give him some speed," Jemima said. Her green eyes flicked over him. "What are you planning, Diamondback?"

"I'm planning to get that woman off that boat. Alive."

"What about the race?"

"It's real simple now. You have to beat him to Sandy Bar."

"But he got a cheatin' jump on me!"

"Looked like a good business move to me. Caught you with your boilers cold."

Jemima's green eyes burned like St. Elmo's fire. "I'll win, Diamondback. I'll show you."

Cord stared back at her. His handsome face was serious. "I'd like to see you win, Jemima. But *you've* got to do it."

"While you're rescuing what's-her-name?"

"I let them kidnap her so the race would go on and you'd have a fighting chance to win. If I'd stopped them in Bell Ridge, Barber would get you later with dynamite, or guns, or whatever else it'd take."

"Mind telling me how you're going to save her?" Jemima said sarcastically.

"Later."

A frown crossed Jemima's face. "You sure are a secretive son of a bitch," she said. "Don't you ever loosen up? Or do you just save it for eastern beauty queens in silk dresses?"

"What do you want to know?" he asked.

"Why are you so hanged in a hurry to get away from the delta? You in trouble here?"

"I just don't like being around a lot of people who are like J. K. Barber."

"People like J. K. Barber are everywhere."

"You're right," Cord admitted. "And I get real tired of them."

"My daddy says that the only way he keeps from goin' crazy is by pretendin' everyone else is a duck. That way, all he hears is a lot of quackin' and he says it sounds pretty funny. He's been tellin' me that ever since I was little. Sometimes I thought he was going to start quackin' back at people. He'd work his mouth like he was goin' to let out a quack, and I'd know what he was thinkin', and I'd laugh my head off."

"Have you been on this river all your life?" Diamondback asked.

"Mostly. We started on the Colorado, down near Yuma. My mother picked up and left us. Daddy thought she'd come up here. We've been here ever since. I think Daddy's still lookin' for her, in a way. Don't know what he'd do if he ever found her, though. She never did appreciate his wildness."

"When did you learn to pilot a steamboat?"

"Hell, I was about four." Jemima giggled and her thick blond hair bobbed in the semidarkness. "Daddy sat me up top of the compass—we were aboard the *Blarney Stone*—and told me what to do. Then he let me take it: I ran us aground. That's where I picked up this scar." She ran a slim finger slowly along the thin white scar that followed her jawline. "When the *Blarney* dragged its bottom, I got thrown through the glass. Daddy always tells me I should be thankful that compass I was perched on didn't follow me out the window or I still wouldn't be able to sit down."

Jemima raised her eyes at the memory. "He lost his job on that one, but he kept teachin' me. By the time I was twelve, I could handle any boat I could see over the bow of.''

Up ahead, the *Westerner* seemed to have stopped opening the gap.

"We're pickin' up speed," Jemima said. "We're startin' to catch them."

"Bad night out there."

"Long as they're ahead, we're all right. Trouble comes when we get alongside and need to see where we're goin'."

"If he lets you get alongside."

"Oh, he won't move over on me," Jemima said confidently. "If he did, he'd risk hitting Sandy Bar himself. The bar could have shifted some. This way, I have to get all the way past him before I can move over. He's already figuring I don't have time to do it."

"Can you make it?"

"Maybe. If we dump that bacon into the fire."

The *Clancy* crept closer to the *Westerner*.

"When are you going to rescue that woman?" Jemima said.

"Soon as we pull alongside."

"What?"

"Barber'll dump her overboard at Sandy Bar, lead or no lead," Cord said. "He can't afford to have her talk. And if she's dead, it'll look as if it's your fault."

"But what are you going to do?"

"Pay a visit to the *Westerner*. I was going to ride with Barber, but Marshal Brake showed up and things happened too fast."

"How do you intend to get over there?" Jemima said.

"Well, I don't have a horse. And I can't swim that fast. Only one way left."

"I suppose you want me to take you over there and let you step across," Jemima said.

"I considered that. I don't think the reception would be too friendly, though."

"Then what else is there?" Jemima demanded.

"What else? I'm going to fly over."

# 19

The stern of the *Westerner* lay only thirty feet to port of the *Clancy*'s bow. The *Clancy* edged forward, jarring over the other boat's wake, gaining slowly.

"Figure they're going to use those rifles?" Jemima asked, pointing toward the *Westerner*'s taffrail. Armed men were poised in the shadows.

"I'd keep my head down," Cord answered.

"Hoodoo, make sure the passengers are off the port side," Jemima ordered.

"Nobody down there," Hoodoo said. "I don't think they're enjoying the view." Opening the gun cabinet at the rear of the pilothouse, near the door to Jemima's cabin, he took down a big Sharps .50-caliber buffalo rifle and dug into the drawer for shells.

"Fixin' to blow her out of the water, Hoodoo?" Jemima said. "Don't go out and start anything."

"Jus' bein' prepared."

Jemima peered ahead. The fog was a soft gray wall, showing nothing.

"I sure hope there's nobody on this river tonight." She tugged the whistle lanyard and the steam shouted its warning into the night.

The starboard door slid open and Arthur Tellock entered the pilothouse. "Looks as if Barber's getting edgy out there. Thought I'd see if you needed any help," he said.

"Stick around," Hoodoo invited.

"What do you know about Barber?" Cord asked the gambler.

"The syphilis is killing him," Tellock said. "Brain's rotting. For a long time, Barber was important in the delta political machine. Buddy-buddy with everybody. Not a bad guy, really. Crooked as hell, but he helped the schools and churches and charities. Then, about a year or two ago, he started sliding downhill. The syphilis started jumbling his mind, made him mean and made him act crazy. Now the machine doesn't know what to do with him. He's a renegade. They all owe him favors, but he's an embarrassment. They're having trouble protecting him. One of these days they're going to let him swing."

"What'll happen if he loses this race?" Cord said.

"They won't lift a finger to help him. They'd love to get him off the river. And Barber knows it. The *Westerner*'s his last chance."

"We're too close to Sandy Bar now," Jemima said tensely. "I don't think I'll be able to get past him."

"How far?"

"Mile and a half, maybe."

"Keep going," Cord urged.

The engineer must have added a barrel of oil, because the *Clancy* spurted ahead, pulling alongside the *Westerner*. Three feet separated the thrashing paddles as they thrust each boat forward to its limits.

"Move closer to them," Cord ordered.

Jemima edged the boat toward the *Westerner*. One wrong move and the two racing steamboats would smash each other into so much scrap lumber.

Not thirty feet away, J. K. Barber stared at Diamondback from the *Westerner*'s hurricane deck, his black eyes penetrating Diamondback's skull like coal miners' drills. He yelled something that Cord couldn't hear over the echoing beat of the sidewheels and shook his fist.

Only two feet separated the two paddlewheels as the *Clancy* fought to inch ahead. Sandy Bar must be less than a mile ahead, Cord calculated. If he didn't force the *Westerner* away, the *Clancy Longborn* was going to drive into the sandbar at full speed.

"Get down!" Hoodoo shouted.

Almost instantly, a wave of gunfire swept over the *Clancy*. The glass windows in the pilothouse shattered and the cold fog swept through.

"Aw, dammit!" Jemima yelled.

The Sharps boomed into the fog from the pilothouse doorway and Hoodoo cackled triumphantly. "Got one of the sons of bitches and took out that runnin' light along with him!"

Now both boats were running blind in the darkness. More rifle shots whistled through the *Clancy*'s pilothouse, digging chips of oiled wood from the bulkheads.

"They'll kill us all if we don't back off," Jemima shouted.

"You handy with anything besides a derringer, Tellock?" Cord asked.

"I can hit the broad side of the *Westerner,* if that's what you mean."

"What's your big plan, Diamondback?" Jemima said impatiently.

"Any chance of you gettin' ahead?" he asked her.

"Sandy Bar's a half mile away. We're gonna plow it up for the rice farmers," she shouted in exasperation. Another volley of rifle fire pelted the wheelhouse.

"Can you handle that rifle, Tellock?" Cord asked, nodding at the Sharps that bucked heavily against Hoodoo's shoulder as he pulled the trigger.

"Damn thing's bigger'n I am," the gambler answered, "but I'll manage."

Cord turned. "Let's go, Hoodoo. Help me out. Jemima, keep an eye on me down below."

The two men headed out the lee side. Cord turned back to the gambler. "I thought your bets were on the *Westerner*."

Tellock braced himself against the powerful recoil of the Sharps before responding. "The betting turned before we got too far out of Bell Ridge. So I started backing the *Clancy*. Better odds. Five to one." He laughed.

Cord signaled Hoodoo to follow.

"What the hell you up to, Diamondback?" Hoodoo said, scuttling up behind him.

"I'm going over there. I want you to swing me over on that forward freight boom."

"Whooo-ee," Hoodoo breathed as they charged down the gangway. "Clancy Longborn would *love* you."

Without warning, Cord was hit from his blind side and smashed into the bulkhead, stunning him. Hard fists drove into his stomach and he sagged toward the deck. The fists quit abruptly and Cord saw Hoodoo pummeling Cord's attacker.

It was Clay Gibbs.

A Hoodoo right snapped Gibbs's nose, taking the fight out of him.

"Goddamn you, Diamondback, where *is* she?" Gibbs snuffled as he flopped against the steps. "Where *is* she?"

"He's drunk," Hoodoo said disdainfully.

Cord pulled himself to his feet, breathing hard.

"Come with us, and I'll show you." They hauled Gibbs to his feet. In the darkness, Cord could see the black streams of blood running from Gibbs's nostrils. The photographer spat it away.

"Let's go," Cord said.

He led them behind the winch on the bottom deck. Shots winged by overhead. Cord looked at Gibbs and pointed at the *Westerner*.

"What's she doing over there?" Gibbs cried disbelievingly.

"Ask her when we get her back."

Gibbs glared at Cord, but the combination of too much whiskey and the shock of the broken nose had knocked the fight out of him.

"What kin I do?" he slurred as he sank back against the base of the winch.

"Keep your head down," Cord said. Gibbs's eyes glazed and he didn't argue.

Barber's men were firing at the *Clancy*'s pilothouse, riddling it with holes. Glass shattered in the darkness three decks overhead. Every few moments the Sharps rifle boomed in return.

Preoccupied with the wheelhouse, Barber's men hadn't seen them sneak behind the heavy winch, which stood almost man tall on the *Clancy*'s main deck. The winch's big drum held hundreds of feet of steel cable. The cable traveled up the forty-foot length of boom, which dangled forward of the *Clancy*'s bow like a big fishing pole. The loop end of the cable was snubbed over a cleat just forward of the winch.

Cord poked his head carefully around the winch, studying the positions of the two boats.

"How far will that boom go to port?"

"Fifteen feet. Twenty, maybe, if it was brought down low," Hoodoo said.

"Keep it up there. I want to reach that pilothouse. We've got to move closer." Cord waved an arm toward Jemima.

"Closer!"

Again the *Clancy* crept toward the *Westerner*. The heavy, driving wakes of the two boats collided, sending waves flooding across the deck.

"Does that boom swing fast?" Cord demanded.

"Purty fast. Not faster'n a bullet, though."

"Swing it as fast as you can."

"What are you going to do—lasso the boat?" Hoodoo said, and spat tobacco into the wave washing around his feet.

"I'm going to hogtie 'em," Cord answered. He dived forward for the cable, tugging the loop end back to the protected spot behind the winch.

Hoodoo engaged the winch. Cord felt the rumble of the drive gears beneath the deck.

"Start drawing in the cable. Swing that boom toward the *Westerner* and at the same time shorten up on the cable. Fast. Crack it like a whip," Cord instructed.

"Run wide," Hoodoo advised. "That cable'll winch fast. I'll pop you right over the bow with the boom. Ready? Now!"

Hoodoo slammed the drive lever forward, engaging the gears. The boom hopped toward the *Westerner*. With a metallic zing the cable began its rapid arc through the night.

Three quick steps forward at full speed and Diamondback was lifted by the rising boom. He felt himself flung outward and upward in a wild arc. In a split second he was sailing toward the *Westerner*'s hurricane deck, his belly floating weightlessly within him. For a moment he thought of his whaling days, the crazy "Nantucket sleigh rides" in the moments after harpooning a big sperm whale when the beast dragged the whaleboat over the ocean swells.

"Get him!" he heard Barber yell, but the bullets pinged through the air around him, missing him. Then he hit. His boots skidded on the mist-dampened deck. Boots thumped toward him along the wood planking as he hit and rolled, his shoulder glancing off the rail. Dazed by the hard fall, Cord pushed himself to his feet and staggered toward the pilothouse.

Cheat Grimes. Barber's thug broke at an angle to him, trying to head him off. As Diamondback tried to fake around him, Grimes reached out. Cord's left fist drove through the man's grasping fingers and he felt it contact Grimes's jaw, snapping the head sideways with a click that sounded like a cue ball doing its work. Grimes flew back against the pilothouse, jolting against the hardwood before collapsing unconscious on the deck.

Hands grabbed Cord roughly. An arm went around his neck, closing off his throat. He struggled, but there were too many of them. He was immobilized.

A big face like a pumpkin leered at him. J. K. Barber laughed. "Very dramatic, Judge, but you're too late! Look!" He jammed a pointing finger forward.

Sandy Bar lay three hundred yards ahead, a blacker spot in the gray night, directly ahead of the *Clancy Longborn*. The *Clancy*'s whistle screamed, sounding as if it were pleading with the *Westerner* to move over.

The *Clancy* suddenly dropped back and Cord could see the whirling buckets of the paddlewheels scratching the river's surface, trying to halt the steamboat's progress. But the *Clancy* plunged onward and a shudder racked the boat as the hull began dragging through the grasping sand.

"There she goes!" Barber bellowed wildly. "So much for the—"

Behind Barber, Cord suddenly saw jagged flaming chunks of the *Westerner*'s midsection lifting into the night. Then the universe howled in his ears until it deafened him.

# 20

Diamondback found himself scrabbling for his balance as the world caught fire around him with the thunderous roar of an exploding volcano. Something white hot skittered across his shoulder blades and he felt blistering pain. Explosions continued like aftershocks. Cord stumbled backward, instinctively trying to avoid the fiery heat from the *Westerner*'s burning midsection.

The boat's boiler had blown itself through the superstructure. Too much overstress for too long had caused the weakened iron to give up. Flaming pieces of metal arced into the night like comets, leaving orange trails of sparks in their wake. Gobs of flaming tar coated the hurricane deck.

The crewman who had been behind Diamondback when the boiler exploded had protected Cord's body with his own from the flying bits of metal and wood. Now he stood bathed in flame, staring sightlessly at the bloody stumps of his hands. No face remained on the still-upright body: it had been scythed away, leaving a cross section of gray brain that began to sizzle and pop in the hot flames. Then it flopped forward, momentarily fanning the flames that slithered toward Diamondback.

145

The *Westerner*'s pilothouse stood far forward, a step ahead of the spreading flames. Chutney was probably still alive, but the fire was working its way from the gaping hole amidships, feeling its way outward in every direction. Heat seared Cord's face.

Someone went into the pilothouse. In the smoke, Cord thought it was Barber. He probably wanted to get Chutney Crane overboard, so that it would look as if she fell off the *Clancy* and drowned in the night's confusion.

On the lower decks of the *Westerner*, people were screaming madly. Cord heard the splashes of people diving overboard as another explosion rocked the aft section of the steamboat.

What had happened to the *Clancy*? As he worked his way forward amid the mangled bodies and burning debris, Cord tried to catch a glimpse of the other boat. Then he saw her.

The *Clancy* was struggling to back off Sandy Bar as the *Westerner* wallowed toward her. Any minute, the ruthless heat from the *Westerner* could set the *Clancy* aflame.

Rescue Chutney. Quickly.

As Cord entered the smoky pilothouse, Barber backhanded the woman journalist as she hugged both arms around the brass compass base.

With a cry of pain, Chutney lunged toward Barber and sank her teeth into the meaty part of his thumb. Barber howled. His other fist rammed her head against the compass. Stunned, Chutney loosened her grip on the compass. Barber ripped her backward with a bleeding hand.

"Don't look now, Barber, but you're losing the race."

Diamondback's voice caught Barber by surprise. He swayed as he turned to look at Cord. One hand remained on the back of Chutney's neck, squeezing hard. The other went inside his coat and came out with a small-caliber Colt revolver.

"The best judge is a dead judge," he said mildly, and fired as Cord threw himself next to a rack that stood behind the bulkhead storage closets leading to Barber's cabin. The round sped harmlessly through the open doorway. The second shot hacked a spray of wood chips from the oak bulkhead.

Barber shoved Chutney away from him and staggered toward Diamondback, the small Colt steadied in both hands.

"Cord! He's coming!" Chutney cried.

Quickly, Cord lifted a small, gimballed compass from the wall rack. With a quick peek, he underhanded the compass hard at Barber and pulled back. One instant later he popped into the open as Barber's gun fired, distracted by the flying object. The compass caught Barber in the mouth as Cord dived at him.

The gun barrel swung to meet him, but Cord brushed it away with a forearm, driving into Barber's chin with his right shoulder. The Colt went off with a deafening roar in the smoky cabin and skittered across the deck.

Barber was tough. The big right paw that had gripped Chutney's neck now clamped over Cord's face, the thick fingers gouging for the eyes. The left swung hard at Diamondback's crotch but it glanced off the thigh.

Cord bit hard into the palm that pressed itself against his mouth, and Barber bellowed in pain. The claws became a fist, battering into the side of Cord's head as the two men crashed into the captain's cabin.

The cabin was in flames. Cord gagged on the acrid smoke as he grappled with Barber.

Momentarily pinning the man's arms, he levered his knees back into the air and then drove them both into the man's fat gut. The air rushed out of Barber with a whuff, and he momentarily loosened his grip.

Flames licked at Barber's hair, and the man shouted, feeling the fire singe him.

The smoke and Barber's punches to his head were making Cord whoozy, but he tugged at Barber's collar. "Don't try anything, Barber, or I'll turn you into a torch."

Barber lumbered to his feet and without stopping tried to hammer Cord into the bulkhead. Cord's left jabbed in with three quick punches that drove Barber back toward the onrushing flames. The burning roof sagged, collapsing slowly toward them.

"Cord! Watch out!" Chutney shouted in fright.

Barber was screaming in pain and fear as he danced out of the fire, now almost unaware of Diamondback. Cord caught him with a right to the chin that crumpled him.

"Cord, leave him. We'll die!" Chutney pleaded. Her face was streaked with black from the oily smoke, and her eye was beginning to swell where Barber had bashed it against the compass housing.

"Get outside," Cord ordered. He began tugging the unconscious man into the wheelhouse, away from the worst of the flames.

"Hurry, Cord!" Chutney begged.

Barber's head bounced over the doorsill like a coconut. The crackling flames were eating away at the pilothouse walls.

"Out, out!" Cord urged Chutney.

They felt the cold air. The *Westerner* had become a bonfire in the darkness. The surging flames threatened to engulf the *Clancy*, which was struggling heroically to back off Sandy Bar. A crewman atop the *Clancy*'s paddle-wheel housing fought to hold the *Westerner* away with a boat hook. Cord could see Hoodoo working the *Clancy*'s huge wheel.

Twenty feet away, Jemima was leaning over the *Clancy*'s rail.

"Jump!" she shouted. "We'll pick you up!" She pointed below, where crewmen were trying to maintain the gap between the two boats, which was six feet at most.

"Get ready," Cord told Chutney. "Hit flat. It's not deep here." He wrestled the still form of J. K. Barber to the rail. Headfirst, the *Westerner*'s owner tumbled toward the water, a leg bouncing off the boat's rail before pancaking into the water.

"Your turn."

Chutney started to protest, but Cord lifted her around her slim waist. "Hit flat," he repeated, and let go. Glancing downward only long enough to make sure he'd miss her, Cord vaulted the rail and punched into the cold water.

It was even shallower than he thought. The hard bottom whammed against his outstretched feet, driving his knees into his chest and knocking the wind out of him. The water was less than four feet deep. He gasped for breath as he tried to get his footing. An outcropping on the bottom raked his ankle painfully.

Chutney, sputtering, was being hauled aboard the *Clancy* by two crewmen. The boat had broken free of Sandy Bar and was beginning to pick up speed in reverse.

Cord reached for Barber's weakly flailing arm and caught hold.

"Get him!" he shouted up to the men on the *Clancy*. Hands grabbed Barber.

"Damn heavy son of a bitch," someone grunted as they struggled to hoist Barber aboard. They moved away with him. There was only one man left at the rail above him.

Clay Gibbs.

Gibbs's booted foot stomped down on Cord's fingers as they gripped the edge of the *Clancy*. A small derringer suddenly appeared.

Diamondback flung himself upward with all the strength left in him. He grabbed Gibbs's boot even as the derringer was aimed at him. Gibbs crashed over the side toward him, smashing down atop him as the derringer went off, its ping lost in the roar of the burning *Westerner*.

Then Gibbs was on top of him, forcing him farther down into the blackness beneath the hull. Hands clamped around Cord's neck.

Cord pushed hard off the shallow bottom and he felt Gibbs's body smack into the hull above them, but the photographer's grip did not relax. Nails dug deeply into Cord's throat, frantically peeling furrows of skin as Gibbs found the soft spot that would close off Cord's windpipe. Cord felt his lungs bursting like two overtaxed boilers as he struggled for a breath, heedless of the black water surrounding them. Air! His own fingers clawed desperately at Gibbs's hands, trying to rip them away.

Then Gibbs himself was out of air, fighting his way to the surface. They came up near the bow of the *Clancy*. The boat was still backing away and the *Westerner* eased closer. Broken wood littered the breach between the two boats.

Cord sucked air. He reached for a splintered sliver of wood the length of a .45. Then his neck snapped sideways as Gibbs flung himself on him.

''Diamondback!'' he heard Hoodoo shout, but he was forced under water again.

This time Gibbs was facing Cord, his hands gripping Cord's throat. Cord drove the wood sliver upward into Gibbs's naked wrist, twisting the frail wood as it pierced the flesh. Gibbs went into a frenzy.

Air! They rode to the surface. Cord's head broke through. His lungs sucked like empty bellows.

He held Gibbs under. Gibbs's hand punched through the surface of the cold water, the bloody splinter still dangling from the meaty part of his forearm. The hands clutched wildly, seeking Cord's eyes, his throat, anything they could get a grip on, but there was nothing.

Gibbs's mad grasping suddenly calmed. The hands relaxed and seemed to float on the surface like two jellyfish.

"Diamondback!" Hoodoo shouted. "Gimme yer hand, boy! Quick!"

"Here," Cord gasped. Exhausted, he pushed Gibbs's unconscious body toward the boat. "Come on, you son of a bitch, wake up and swim," he mumbled. He felt as if he were trying to push the man up a raging river.

"Let him go, Diamondback," Hoodoo urged. "We're backin' away from the bar. The *Westerner*'s drifting in here!"

"No. Get him!" Diamondback breathed. With a giant heave, he sent Gibbs within reach of the old man.

"Swim, Diamondback, swim," Hoodoo begged as he struggled to lift Gibbs's inert body aboard.

Cord was sucking in water. He felt as if he could no longer keep his head above the surface. Two more strokes. His arms lifted like lead rods. He sensed the *Clancy* slipping away from him.

Then there was a hand on his collar, pulling at him. Cord felt himself tugged aboard as the *Clancy* freed itself from the clutches of the Sandy Bar and the *Westerner*. Burning embers from the *Westerner*'s carcass floated onto the *Clancy*.

Then the *Clancy* was out of range.

# 21

"Keep looking," Jemima ordered the crewman. "There may be more survivors. If you find any, bring them in here."

"Right, Cap'n." He hurried out the doors to his starboard watch station.

Cord surveyed the scene before him.

Jemima had turned the saloon into an infirmary. Burned and scalded victims of the *Westerner* explosion were lying on white mattresses scattered around the elaborately furnished room with its gilt-edged drapes and stained-glass windows. Blood seeped into the wine-colored carpet, screams echoed under the vaulted ceiling. With the electric lamps damaged, candles had been brought in, and an eerie yellow light reflecting from the copper and brass fixtures illuminated the hellish spectacle.

"Tellock's dead." Jemima pointed to a still form in the middle of the saloon. The body was covered by a gray frockcoat. Jemima's voice caught.

"How? Did they shoot him?"

Jemima nodded. "They picked him off right after you jumped over to the *Westerner*. Caught him right through the throat. He lay there gurgling and twitching and there wasn't a damn thing I could do about it."

Cord didn't say anything. Tellock could easily have stayed below decks, safe from the gunfire. Instead he had fought back.

"He was a friend of my daddy's," Jemima said. She swept her tired face with her hand, as if to brush away memories. "Got to leave soon," she told Cord. "Can't spend any more time searching. There's no doctor aboard. We've got to get these people to Sacramento. Done all we can for them, here."

Her face was haggard with the strain of the past twenty-four hours. The green eyes looked washed out and sleepy and the coffee mug she carried was shaking visibly.

"Are you going to make it, Jemima?"

"Me? 'Course I'll make it," she bristled. "What about you? Hell, you've been a fightin' fool tonight, and you've got that burn across your back. I should charge you for providin' you with so much excitement."

"What will you charge to let me get some sleep?" Diamondback smiled.

The woman's mouth swept into a wide grin that seemed to burn away some of his tiredness.

"Nothing. Long as I get some too," she said. " 'Course, you'll probably find you don't have any mattress on yer bed. Most of 'em are in here. I ordered my crew to bring down as many mattresses as needed. May've lost mine too."

"This is your deluxe run, I take it," Cord said.

Jemima laughed. "Terrific, huh? You should ride downriver with us sometime."

"Love to."

"I—" She was interrupted by someone waving to her from the saloon doors. "Dammit, what now? Time to head for Sacramento. Look at these poor people. You know, the way I feel at this moment, if I didn't see a riverboat again, I wouldn't care. You play with 'em too hard and they turn on you eventually and kill you. Never fails.'' They left the saloon, heading for the pilothouse.

"Aw, hell, there's Brake.''

Jemima nodded at the dock where the marshal stood with two other men. Deputies, from the looks of them, Cord decided. They looked sleepy, as if Brake had roused them when he reached Sacramento.

"He sure must've hurried to beat us up here,'' Cord observed.

"Wouldn't have been here to meet us if we hadn't stopped,'' Jemima said. She moved to the rail of the main deck.

"Ike, get yer butt into town for some doctors and some litter wagons,'' she directed. "Gilly, you and the others start arranging those people out here on the deck so we can move 'em more quickly.''

Brake climbed the landing stage looking as if he were sore from riding hard. The deputies followed him.

As he reached them, Brake casually eased the Colt Model 1873 .45 revolver from the holster on his hip and directed it at Cord.

"You, Diamondback, and the lady here are under arrest,'' he said without preliminaries. "And so is Barber. Where is he?''

"Wait a minute,'' Jemima protested. "What the hell do you mean, you're arresting us? What for?''

"Murder. Manslaughter. River racing. Conspiracy. Got a boatload of charges that'll stick. Pick one.''

"What are you talkin' about, murder,'' Jemima raged, pushing close to Brake and staring up into his face.

"Gonna be a grand jury investigatin' your trip,'' Brake

said. "Seems like an awful lot of hurt people for a peaceful little trip upriver."

"Dammit, we simply picked up survivors from the *Westerner* when her boiler exploded and sprayed people all over the river."

"The *Westerner* was supposed to be on her downriver run."

"Sounds about right for Barber," Jemima snorted. "I'm supposed to know what the *Westerner* is doing?"

"Look, don't give me any more of your lip, lady," Brake commanded. "I said, you and Diamondback and Barber are goin' to jail. *Now*." The Colt moved menacingly from Cord to Jemima and Brake's jaw muscles bunched under his black beard. "Now come on, where's Barber?"

Jemima tossed her head upward toward the promenade deck. "In the Grand Saloon, with the busted leg he got from jumpin' off his boat."

"Let's go." Brake urged her forward with the gun.

"I've got a boatload of injured people, and I sure as hell don't intend to leave until—"

"Lady, shut up," Brake warned, his lips pulling back over the big yellow teeth as he poked the Colt's barrel into her side. "I don't care what you intend, you're goin' to jail."

"Aren't you goin' to do somethin' about this?" Jemima demanded, looking at Cord. "You're a judge."

Cord shrugged.

"I wouldn't try *anything*, Diamondback," Brake said quickly. The barrel of the Colt swung back.

"Hey, I'm not causing any problems for you," Cord said, raising his hands as if to assure Brake that he was harmless. He moved off in the direction Brake indicated with the barrel of his gun.

"You river rats are all the same," Brake complained to Jemima as he herded them into the saloon. "Killin' and maimin' people, and then whining about how tough it is to make it on the river. Burns my ass."

Cord scanned the saloon-turned-hospital. He saw Barber lying on a mattress against the far wall. Barber turned over, faking sleep, when he spotted them. A rough splint tied with strips of checkered cloth encased his left leg.

Where was Chutney? She had been methodically working her way among the survivors of the *Westerner,* interviewing them, putting together a story about their ordeal. When Cord was brought aboard the *Clancy,* she had flitted by, barely noticing him in her hungry quest for more first-hand accounts of the disaster.

"Trouble, Mr. Diamondback?" The Boston accent came from behind him. "Did you rob the *Clancy's* safe, or something equally awful?" Alive with the energy from the news scoop that was hers and hers alone, Chutney fluttered through the somber scene like a butterfly at a funeral.

"Marshal Brake here feels compelled to put us in jail for saving people from the *Westerner,*" Cord said.

"Shut up," Brake snarled. "You don't talk to anybody but your lawyer and the grand jury."

Cord's guess was accurate. Chutney's eyes went a darker shade of gold as she realized that the story behind her scoop was becoming even more complicated. More story possibilities. She immediately buttonholed the marshal.

"I'm sorry, sir, we haven't met. I'm Chutney Crane of the New York *Daily Intelligencer*—I was aboard the *Westerner* when the explosion occurred." Chutney extended her hand toward Brake.

"A lady reporter? Look, lady, I don't have time now," Brake said. He was irritated.

"But I'd like to discuss your role in this whole affair—"

"*Beat it!*" Brake roared. "Get the hell out of here or I'll pull you in too!" He turned away from the woman. "Where the hell is Barber?"

"Right here, Marshal," Jemima indicated.

"Get him up. Let's go, Barber." Brake nudged Barber testily with the toe of his boot.

"I got a damn broken leg," Barber complained.

"Tough."

Chutney was hanging close, and Cord could see from the look in her eyes that she was filing away every detail of the scene.

"Get him up," Brake ordered the two deputies. Barber yowled as they pulled him off the mattress, his bad leg dangling uselessly. Shiny beads of sweat spotted his round face, and he bit his lip to keep from crying out.

"Okay," Barber said. The three lawmen prodded their prisoners, Cord helping Barber to hobble along.

Cord looked over at Chutney as he was pushed forward. His dark eyes glittered in the light of the oil lamps and he saw her frown in thought.

"Big story here," he reminded her as he passed.

"I said *shut up*, Diamondback!" Brake's left fist drove hard into Cord's kidney and he staggered ahead with Barber's weight, almost falling over a badly burned Chinaman who lay moaning on a bloody mattress. Pus oozed from the charred holes where the man's eyes had been.

Cord looked back at Brake, whose lip had curled in disgust at the sight of the burned man. "See, Diamondback," he said. "Somebody's going to pay for that. I'm going to make sure it's you three."

"Why? So you can get the railroad onto the river?" Barber said. He laughed harshly and the ugly crusted sore under his nose split and began to bleed.

"Don't worry about it, Barber," Brake answered. "They'll hang you and these two. It doesn't matter a shit who'll be on that river. You three will be dead meat."

# 22

---

Chutney was pacing back and forth outside the Sacramento jail. Cord rolled his shoulders under his coat as he walked toward her, trying to work out some of the kinks from a day and night in the tiny cell. The pain from the burn across his shoulder blades had settled to a dull, steady ache. He owed Brake for this one.

His rugged face was serious under the brown Stetson as he came face-to-face with the reporter.

"Thanks."

"No thanks involved," Chutney said. "I had a first-person scoop and I ran with it—right over to the Sacramento *Western Statesman*. They printed it this morning. All of Sacramento already knows about the bravery and heroism of Cord Diamondback and Captain Jemima Longborn. Sorry it couldn't have been yesterday, so you didn't have to spend the night. But even if the story had run yesterday morning, I don't think it would have done much good."

"Why not?"

"I guess Marshal Brake had some time to put that dim little brain of his to work. By the time my story broke, he was half inclined to release you and the captain anyway.

Seems as if he's mainly after Barber, although I haven't yet been able to discover why."

"I guess he cooled off," Cord said.

"When he saw the stories, he decided to let you two go. I mean, you and the captain are practically the king and queen of the Sacramento."

"No thanks to your story, right?"

"Well, I admit it's a tad laudatory. But the *Intelligencer* would pump it up. *Will* pump it up. I've already sent it east. They'll love it. Between you and Jemima Longborn, I've got stories for weeks."

"What'd you say about Barber?" Cord adjusted the Stetson on his head as he scanned the street. Sacramento seemed to have grown since the last time he'd seen it. Wagons loaded with goods were bustling along the dirt street in a steady stream and a rapid pulse of squeaking wheels and loud voices dinned in his ears as the draymen argued right-of-way.

"I wrote that Barber and his gang of thugs deserve everything they will get. I don't take to being held captive by a bunch of penny-ante crooks. That goon Cheat Grimes was killed in the explosion. Barber, I'm not sure about. Somebody was in the jailhouse screaming about getting him out. Maybe they'll let him loose, despite Brake."

"So you think you were kidnapped by a bunch of two-bit hoodlums?" Cord said. "Chutney, you're not taking it far enough."

"What do you mean?" Chutney demanded, cocking her head unconsciously.

"I mean that what happened on that river was only the tip of the story. Barber is part of the same political machine that Billy Fallows ran. The machine didn't die with Fallows. Half the politicians and judges in Sacramento and San Francisco keep it going. You're in a hell of a position to bust it open. The papers out here are scared to death of the delta machine, as they call it. If they tried to start anything, they'd be burned out. Literally. But you could unravel it through the New York papers and all the papers out here would pick it up.''

''Why should anyone back East care about California politics?''

''Why should they care about Christopher Deacon?'' Cord countered. ''Because the same sleazy characters are involved and you'll get all the sensation you want. Think about it—murder, prostitution, arson, fear among the citizenry. And not pure sensationalism. It's complex. The kind of journalism you told me you were interested in doing.''

''And what would you want out of it?'' she asked shrewdly.

''I don't want my name mentioned or my picture taken.''

Her small mouth creased upward. ''The only person in the world who doesn't want publicity.''

Cord shrugged.

''I'm still thinking about the whole thing, Cord,'' Chutney said, facing him squarely and looking up into his handsome face. The golden eyes sparkled in the sunlight. ''Christopher Deacon is still too hot a story to pass up. I just don't know.''

Cord glanced up and down the street. He had a sudden vision of himself on the run again, trying to fit into a new identity, one that didn't include either judging or fighting. He could either start running right now or move slowly and hope and pray Chutney was able to subdue the news beast within her.

''I'd be a dead man if you do that story about me.''

''But we both know that Billy Fallows was a crook,''

Chutney protested. "It'd come out in a trial, with the information you've given me. They'd never convict you!"

"It wouldn't come to a trial. There's a bounty on me, dead or alive. And dead, I'm much more manageable."

"But you could turn yourself in!"

"And when they found out what I knew and you knew about the delta machine, how long do you think I'd last? How long do you think *you'd* last?"

"They wouldn't kill a reporter!" Chutney huffed. "Every reporter in the country would be swarming out here."

"They wouldn't? What were they going to do with you the other night? Hold a birthday party?"

The golden eyes looked at him, stricken. "You're right," she muttered. "It doesn't make me want to stop with the Christopher Deacon story, but I want to tackle the machine. Got my very own Tammany Hall to break!"

"Watch yourself," he warned. "A lot of people out here aren't concerned how pretty you are. A pile of bank notes stacked in front of them might look a lot prettier."

"What are you talking about?" she demanded. The golden eyes narrowed.

"Just be careful."

She left it at that and there was silence.

"What's your buddy Gibbs up to?" Cord asked.

"You worked him over pretty well. He deserved it too, the fool. He's mostly just moping around the *Clancy*, playing with his cameras. Wants to get out of here and go back to New York, but I told him he had to wait until I got my stories."

"You keep him wrapped just tightly enough around your finger so that he's manageable, right?"

"I do *not*!" she protested angrily. "What right do you have to say that? Just because you got what *you* wanted, Mr. Stud Diamondback? I'm getting out of here!"

She briefly tugged at her silk skirt and short jacket. "Your precious captain should be right out."

As she said it, the door of the jail pushed open and Jemima walked toward them impassively. She was still in the denims and leather coat they'd taken her away in.

"Well, here comes Cleopatra of the delta," Chutney said sardonically. "Time to go." She waved at an oncoming hansom cab and the driver urged his horse toward them.

"Congratulations, Captain," Chutney said brightly. "Glad you got out of that awful place."

"Thanks."

"Well, I'm off. I'll talk to you later, Captain. I'd like to get some of your impressions."

"Right."

The hansom clattered off, leaving Cord and Jemima alone.

"How are you?" he asked.

"What was that all about?"

"She did a story for the Sacramento paper. It helped get us out. Of course, we are now heroes. There's a certain burden that goes with being a hero."

"Such as?"

"Just you wait," he warned. "Now that they've heard about the exploits of Jemima Longborn, the *Clancy* will be loaded to the gunwales with rubberneckers who want to see the Queen of the Sacramento."

"What are you talking about?" Jemima asked suspiciously.

"Chutney offered the gist of her story to me. She's calling you the Queen of the Sacramento River. Said that the article will have men flocking out here in droves, looking to tame the fiery female captain of the *Clancy Longborn*."

"Oh, terrific," she said, but he could see the idea intrigued her.

She shook her head and the blond hair paled to silver with the morning sunlight behind it. The green eyes locked onto his own.

"What about you?" she said. "Care to be the first in line for the Queen of the Sacramento, Judge?"

"Can't think of anything I'd like better."

"Sittin' in that jail, I began to wonder if you were good at anything besides fightin'. I can't say much about the peaceful nature of your judgin'."

Without another word, she turned and walked away in the direction of the river. He stood for a moment and admired the small, firm body moving so confidently.

They were out of jail, but Cord doubted they were home free. If Barber had the chance, he'd keep trying to finish them both off. Only, how would he try to do it? And when?

# 23

"How are you going to like all the publicity?" Cord asked.

"I get the boat down the river. I get the boat up the river. How I do it is nobody's business but my own." Jemima slid off her denims in a single motion, revealing firm, straight legs. Her naked ass was hard, her thighs showed well-defined muscles as she turned to throw the denims over the battered oak straightback chair in the corner of the small cabin. Quickly, she fiddled with the stove, lighting match after wooden match to the balky pilot light.

Official certificates hung down the patch of wall next to the bed, topped by her pilot's license and the *Clancy*'s operating permit. An electric lamp stood atop the end table, and a brochure entitled "Alaska: World of Wealth" lay next to it. Two photographs of the *Clancy* under way, and one of a hawk-nosed man with bushy gray eyebrows and a big grin decorated the bulkhead next to the plain oak chest of drawers.

"Is that your father?"

"That's Daddy, all right. Keepin' watch over me."

"Where did you stay when your father was around?"

"This was always my cabin. Daddy slept in the crew's quarters. Or with the ladies. Never seemed to mind too much about not having his own spot."

The stove was going and she dived for the narrow double bed. "Move over, Diamondback. Till this damn stove heats up, this cabin's gonna be colder than the bottom of San Francisco Bay."

Even as she was scrambling under the covers he cupped his big hand over the patch of blond pubic hair flashing by him. He felt the warm lips of her vagina slip between his fingers.

"Hurry, Diamondback, get those damn stovepipes and that shirt and those pants off, and get under here!" she urged.

Cord quickly peeled off everything but the flannel shirt. No need for her to know, even if she was one person in the world who would applaud what he had done to Billy Fallows.

"What about the shirt?"

"What about it?"

"How am I going to admire the muscles that conquered Bobo the Bear if you're not going to take off your shirt."

"No muscles under," Cord said. "Just a bunch of tiny sandbags built into my shirt so I look tough. I wouldn't want the word to get around."

Jemima giggled. "Suit yourself," she said, and kissed him. Her tongue probed deep into his mouth and he sucked on it, feeling his penis rise.

Jemima felt it too as she lay full length on top of him. She scissored her legs around his stiff cock and reached behind her to run a finger softly over the trapped head. Then, more insistently, she pulled it up against her. Unlocking her legs, she popped up quickly. Her hands glided down his flanks and returned to his crotch. Then her tongue was out, licking his balls as she cupped them in both hands.

Cord slid his hands down to the firm breasts that were caressing his thighs as her tongue climbed the hard pole of his penis. The small pink nipples stiffened as he squeezed them gently and Jemima moaned with pleasure. Her mouth sank down on his penis, warm and deep.

"Wait."

His two powerful arms rotated the small body and he pushed his face into the golden downy softness between her legs. Using his elbows, he spread her legs wide and pushed his face hard against her, feeling the juice of her excitement sluice over the bridge of his nose and his chin as he slid his tongue deep into her.

With a cry, she reached behind his neck with both hands, struggling to pull his mouth farther into her, even as she sought to take every inch of him into her mouth.

He fought himself, struggled to stop the onrushing burst of ecstasy that was coming, but Jemima's insistent mouth made it impossible. Suddenly, he was thrusting into her and she was gulping his sperm, tasting the hot rush that raced out of him in thumping spasms. He sank his face back into her, swinging his face so that his cheeks glistened with the sweet sharpness of her as she strained against his arms. Then she bellowed in triumph even as she sucked him.

"More!" she ordered as she pulled off him, licking away the last spasm of his juice.

He turned her, lifted her.

"Where's it goin'?" she moaned frantically as she watched his penis drooping after its effort.

"Encourage it," Cord advised, smiling.

She straddled him, gently trying to cram his softened organ into her.

"It's not working," she moaned.

"No?"

Sure enough, he was beginning to harden, his urgency rising to meet hers.

"Oh, yeah, yeah, yeah," she breathed as she felt him grow within her.

She crouched over him, balanced on the balls of her feet, her hands grasping her shins. She began bobbing up and down, the slippery friction of his hard penis in her vagina their only contact. Her eyes were slits, the pale green rims fastened on him in some private, intense inner pleasure.

Suddenly, he reached out and arrested her bobbing. A throaty growl of frustration came from the wide mouth. Cord slipped his arms between her spread knees, his forearms pressed up against the smooth backs of her legs, a big, muscular hand cupping each small buttock.

"I want—"

"Shut up," he said. His strong arms lifted her; she remained in her crouch and in a moment her feet were off the bed. She was suspended by his arms. He lowered her slowly until his shaft was buried deeply in her and he could feel and see the blond crotch hairs mingling with his own. He raised his arms slowly, lifting her into the air, and he slid out of her, very slowly, until only the very tip of his penis remained in her.

Jemima inhaled sharply, her eyes shut, her being centered on that tiny point of contact.

Suddenly he was a human machine gun; his penis entered her, its throbbing head moving in and out rhythmically.

"Oh, deeper, deeper. Hurry!" The wide mouth opened and Jemima rolled her head back, the thick blond curls bobbing under the shocks of his rapid-fire thrusts. "Hurry, hurry, hurry, you bastard!" she demanded, but he was already plunging deeply into her, his pelvis slamming against the backs of her thighs, battering her into an earthquake of ecstasy.

"Yes, yes, yes," Jemima chanted, praying for the on-rushing wave, but he raised her again, teasing her with the tip of his penis now. He couldn't stand it anymore, his need was a tidal bore heading upriver. But he held her and then rapped into another staccato of pumping

"Now, goddammit, now!" Jemima swung her fists at him, wild roundhouse punches that glanced off his muscled upper arms like pebbles bouncing down a mountain's face.

He dropped her onto him, pulled her down, fitting her atop him like two parts of a puzzle, hammering into her with sledge hammer thrusts.

"Ahhhhhhh!" Her wail of ultimate pleasure filled the small cabin, echoed by and mixed with Diamondback's. She dropped against him, spent, and he wrapped his arms around her, enveloping the tiny body. He pulled up the covers.

"What's your crew going to think of that?"

"Usually not an issue. The engines cover up. I don't think any engines are going to cover this up, though." She laughed. "Maybe no one's around."

"Too much to hope for."

"Why do you keep your shirt on?" she asked. "It's hot in here now."

"I got burned when the *Westerner* exploded."

"Are you okay?"

"Yeah."

"Let me look at it. I can put a little salve on it—"

"No."

Hurt by his abruptness, she turned away.

"I'm sorry," he said. "My back's fine. My knuckles

aren't so good." He showed her his scarred hands. "Now if I could just put some ball bearings in there instead of bone . . ."

She giggled.

Suddenly someone was hammering at the door of the cabin.

"Come on out, Captain." It was Brake's voice. He rapped again.

"I'm free, remember, Brake?" Jemima said, raising her voice.

"How long you stay free is up to me," Brake countered. "I want to talk to you."

Jemima's eyes flickered toward Diamondback. "What do you figure he wants?" she said quietly.

"Make your life miserable."

"Open it up, Longborn, or *I'll* open it," Brake threatened.

"I'm comin', I'm comin."

"Well, make it quick." Brake said it as if he needed something to say.

Jemima slid her jeans on and quickly did the buttons up the front. Her breasts were proportioned to her small body, Cord realized, but they looked bigger.

She noticed his attention. A smile flickered over the wide mouth and disappeared as she pulled on her shirt.

"You stayin'?"

"No," he said. He tugged on his pants and boots.

She opened the door. Marshal Brake pushed himself off the bulkhead where he was leaning. He looked at Jemima and then at Cord. A leer flickered briefly, showing the yellow teeth.

"Good. Now I don't have to go chasin' Diamondback."

"What's goin' on?" Jemima demanded.

"Where's Barber?"

"How the hell would I know?" Jemima exploded. "Ain't he in jail?"

"Some of his political friends got him sprung. The locals caved in under pressure. Figured they could override the arrest made by a marshal."

"Why would he be here?" Jemima demanded.

"I'm still not convinced you ain't all in cahoots."

"What do you need, Marshal?" Cord suddenly asked.

"I don't *need* anything," Brake spat. "When I need something, I don't go to a phony judge for help."

"Why should he need anything from us?" Jemima said to Cord.

Cord stared levelly at the bearded marshal as he spoke to Jemima.

"I've got a hunch that a little good publicity about Brake dismantling the delta machine wouldn't hurt his career any. Particularly if he thought he might be senator material. It'd keep him in good with his railroad buddies."

Brake's eyes widened a hair. "The railroad doesn't own me," he said harshly.

"Maybe not," Cord said, although his dark eyes showed he didn't believe it. "But Chutney Crane could spread your name up and down both coasts," Cord continued. "And you know what that means out here: you get a good chance to break the delta machine's back. Make it easier and cheaper for the railroad to operate, and easier for them to raise rates."

"So I'll owe Chutney Crane. Where do you fit in?"

"I don't. Jemima does. She's a hero. She stays on the river. Last big riverboat on the Sacramento. Memory of the good old days. And she doesn't cut into railroad profits much. She'd need your support to keep operating."

"They're greedy people."

"But with your help they'll see that it's in their best

interests to promote California's glamorous past. Brings people out here, right?''

Brake nodded. "I get you. But I still can't figure out how you benefit from all this, Diamondback. I'm real curious.''

Cord smiled. "A free-lance judge needs business opportunities, Marshal. A little publicity doesn't hurt at all.''

"I thought so, Diamondback. I thought so.'' He shook his head. "How do I get this so-called publicity?''

"Barber's already pushed Chutney Crane around enough. She's looking to push back. Hard. All you have to do is talk to her.''

Brake ran his thumb along his jawline, sliding it slowly over the bristles of his beard.

"Okay, Diamondback. I'm ready to go after Fallows' old cronies, and I'll start with Barber. But if I don't get that newspaper support, and quickly, I'll shut this boat down, and I'll come looking for you. The delta machine won't have time to get to you first, I assure you.''

Diamondback shrugged. "Fair enough.''

"In the meantime, I'm sure they'll be lookin' for you two. I wouldn't go too far from this boat, if I was you.''

"Wouldn't think of it, Marshal, wouldn't think of it,'' Diamondback agreed.

# 24

Hoodoo had volunteered to "fix some grub," as he put it, for the four of them that night. The rest of the crew had gone into Sacramento for some action.

"Whoooo-ee," the old man whistled admiringly as he tapped his biscuits out of the pan onto the plates. "Look at them little beauties. Let's eat."

They had fixed the electrical system that afternoon and the saloon was brightly lit.

"Two hundred seats ought to be enough for the four of us, don't you think, Diamondback?" Jemima asked with a smile on her wide mouth, and Hoodoo cackled with glee.

"Five."

Chutney Crane led the way into the galley, followed by Clay Gibbs. "I insisted that Clay come tonight to demonstrate that he is capable of better behavior than he has previously exhibited. Do you mind?" She searched their faces.

"Him promisin' to be good is like a rattler rattlin'," Hoodoo opined half under his breath.

"Hoodoo, be quiet," Jemima said. "If he's willing to be friendly, we're willing to have him." Her eyes were wary.

Gibbs and Chutney had both dressed for the dinner, Chutney in another dress of pale blue taffeta with a pale yellow weave in it that highlighted her golden eyes. Gibbs wore a black evening jacket over a white pleated shirt, with a black cravat.

The other three, still in their rougher clothes, looked at each other.

"Didn't know I was supposed to be so fancy-dancy," Hoodoo muttered.

"Gibbs, why don't you pour the wine?" Jemima suggested. "Red and white over there in those decanters." Gibbs was actually sweating, although the saloon was on the cool side, with so few people providing body heat in the big hall.

"Whiskey for me," Hoodoo stuck in. "That wine'll rot yer gut and kill ya."

They laughed.

"Well, we're settlin' for leftovers tonight," Hoodoo said with satisfaction. "We got leftover shrimp and crab, leftover cavy-yar, and leftover filet migg-non. I hope you ain't disappointed that you're gettin' leftovers."

"Sounds great, Hoodoo," Chutney said. She must have been hungry, because she sounded as if she meant it.

The food looked wonderful to Cord. He realized that he hadn't eaten much in the last two days, and he thought he could still feel the slightly metallic taste of the mouthful of garlic cloves he'd chewed three nights before for Bobo's benefit. Never again.

Gibbs passed around the wineglasses without a word, his eyes glittering as he handed one to Diamondback.

"A toast," Chutney offered, raising her glass. "To the delta machine—only briefly may it reign."

"Attaway," Hoodoo added.

Gibbs tossed off his glass of wine and poured himself another.

"A bit anxious, aren't you, Clay?" Chutney commented.

"No." Gibbs second glass of wine followed the first.

The food began making its way to the plates.

"We still haven't talked about what we can do to protect ourselves against Barber and the machine," Chutney said as she cracked a thick crab's leg. "I found out a lot today from Brake, enough to base an article on. Which I finished and telegraphed east. Tomorrow I'll be pursuing some other leads which should pay off very quickly."

Cord watched as Gibbs morosely downed his third glass of wine.

"Until Brake gets some legal action going against members of the machine, we can't do anything but keep our heads down. And be ready for anything." He nodded toward a corner of the saloon. Three carbines were propped against the wall, with several boxes of cartridges sitting on a chair close by.

"You don't seriously think they'll try a shoot-out, do you, Mr. Diamondback?" Chutney said in disbelief. "I mean, we're right in the middle of Sacramento."

"I don't know. Will they, Gibbs?"

Gibbs snapped his attention from the carbines. His eyes bounced dazedly away from contact with any of them.

"What are you talkin' about?"

"I'd guess that you *know* we're going to be paid a visit tonight by Barber and his friends."

Gibbs angrily flung an arm toward Diamondback, knocking over the remains of his fourth glass of wine. "You're right, Diamondback, I know they're coming. I let them know you'd be here!"

"But why, Clay?" Chutney asked, stricken.

"Why not? I'm sick of you ignoring me, except when you want something," Gibbs ranted drunkenly at her. "And I don't have to take it when some dirty cowboy drags you out in the bushes for a moonlight fuck, and you go along with it. Then you tell me to get lost, like some kind of serving maid. You can go to hell!'' He shoved Chutney, scattering the meal onto the floor as the woman was driven against the table.

Gibbs staggered toward the door of the saloon.

''As far as Diamondback goes, I missed twice, but I won't miss again. Got help this time. As soon as I'm off this boat, they'll come visit. By then, I'll be headed back East.''

''As soon as they spot you, they'll start firing,'' Diamondback said as he bolted for the carbines. They won't take any chances, letting you go.''

Gibbs was quivering. ''You're wrong. I gave them Chutney's notes. They know I'm square.''

''Hoodoo, get the lights! Here!'' Cord tossed the old man one of the Winchesters.

''Whoooo-ee!'' Hoodoo whistled. ''Didn't even finish my damn whiskey!''

Jemima picked up the second carbine.

''Chutney! Stay away from those windows!'' Cord hissed. He grabbed her arm and pulled her down to the carpet.

Suddenly shots erupted from the shore and the window where Chutney had been standing exploded inward, spraying them with shards of glass. The lights went out and they were in darkness.

Cord heard the quiet click of a revolver. Inside. A half-dozen feet to his left.

Gibbs was armed.

Where was he? In the darkness, everyone was silent. Feet could be heard running up the landing stage and into the *Clancy*.

He had to move fast to stop them. But if he moved,

Gibbs would shoot. And he couldn't tell if Chutney was in between them.

Silently he slipped his knife from the top of his boot. Raising his carbine, he leveled it to where the revolver had clicked.

He threw the knife, clattering it along the nearest row of chairs.

Gibbs fired. A long white flame jetted from the revolver in the darkness, firing toward the knife.

Cord fired the carbine, pumping shots at Gibbs. The man screamed and crashed into the chairs around him.

Chutney screamed. Feet pounded along the promenade deck.

"Chutney, stay down!" Cord ordered. "Jemima, Hoodoo, pick off who you can!"

He sprinted up the wide staircase to the saloon as more shots erupted, smashing chandeliers.

He had to circle them, whoever was aboard. Five or six guns, he estimated, from the sound of it. And somewhere out there was J. K. Barber with his broken leg, waiting.

Gunfire exploded from below and Cord heard a scream. A body dropped over the side, bumped through the narrow space between the boat and the wood pilings, and splashed into the water.

Footsteps raced along the deck below. Cord could hear them working their way two steps at a time in the stairwell where he was crouched. Barber's man reached the top stair and Cord shot him, blasting a hole in the man's chest and driving him back down the stairs. His rifle clattered down the well alongside him and stopped.

Two.

They were in trouble if Barber's goons got behind them. But Barber had only a few minutes to wipe them out before the Sacramento police arrived to find out what the shooting was all about.

Cord peered around the corner of the stairwell, looking toward shore. Twenty-five yards away a figure limped through the gloom and stopped behind some bales of cotton. The figure propped a rifle against the top one. Cord saw the barrel, a dark shadow against the white of the cotton.

Barber.

The Winchester was a good gun. From twenty-five yards, Barber would be a dead man. But it was dark and only Barber's head showed indistinctly over the cotton bale like a bud on a tree branch.

Barber fired, and there was a scream from below. A woman's scream.

Jemima.

Cord lifted the Winchester and aimed carefully. There. Barber's head and shoulder were above the bale, sighting for his next shot. Cord fired.

Barber's head dissolved in the darkness, the round black spot melting into flitting black things that flew outward and disappeared.

The sudden silence became a patter of boot leather as Barber's men realized there was no point in hanging around.

One. Two. Three. They were all racing down the landing stage at the same time. Cord picked off the leader. At the same moment there was a report from below and the third man dropped. The second man, alone now, spun around. Cord could almost feel his panic.

The Winchester spoke loudly. The last man flopped backward over the rail, bouncing with a broken pumpkin sound onto the granite of the pier.

"Hee, hee, hee," came Hoodoo's cackle from below. "Nice shootin', Diamondback. Now get down here and help Jemima."

# 25

---

"Well, they're not likely to shoot at you anymore," Brake said to Jemima in a satisfied tone. "We've gotten too many of them now. They're going to be running scared. Every one of 'em will be hoping he doesn't get connected with the delta machine."

Jemima fooled with the cloth sling holding her right arm. Barber's bullet had punched a hole in her shoulder, chipping the collarbone but missing everything else. In a month she'd be okay, but she could expect to be able to predict rain from the ache in her shoulder, Cord suspected.

"Where does that leave me?" Jemima asked Brake.

"I'm going to be busy rounding up the machine for quite a while. Helping the grand juries and all. They set up two grand juries yesterday, and I expect one more. To consider corruption in state government. I guess there ain't any steamboats left to race on the Sacramento, so I guess there's no point in arrestin' you."

"Great."

"And people I talked to said the *Clancy* probably had a long future on the Sacramento. Quaint, they call it. Seems as how several of the Big Four occasionally like to get off their trains and enjoy a little jaunt up the river once in a while. You lucked out.''

"Right.''

Brake turned to Cord. "You're out of my hair too, Diamondback. You spill a lot of blood, wherever you go, so I prefer you not to show up here too often. Your kind ain't too much longer for California. You're out-of-date. Free-lance judge.'' Brake spat contemptuously. "Looks like gunslingin' to me. Hope I can prove it some day.''

"Thanks for the warning, Marshal.''

Chutney Crane took in Brake's words from the top of the gangway.

"Let's go, Marshal,'' she encouraged. "We've got one more interview for my story about you, to reconstruct the notes Clay stole. Then I've got a train to catch.''

"Yes, ma'am. I'll bring up the carriage.'' Brake thumped toward the dock.

"Power of the press.'' Chutney winked. "Especially with aspiring politicians. Well, time to go. Captain Longborn, it has been interesting. Hoodoo.'' She started down the gangway with Cord behind her.

"Will that hold you for a while?''

Chutney didn't respond immediately to Cord's question. She looked out over the rail of the gangway, a smile flickering on her lips.

"The story of the evil men of the Sacramento Steamboat Company and what they tried to do to a lovely lady steamboat captain. New York is already eating this up.'' She turned to Cord and suddenly her golden eyes were serious. "It'll hold me for a while, Cord.''

He didn't say anything.

"Of course,'' she said, "I'll expect periodic reports on the state of the West. You'll be my inside source for a lot of good stories. Don't think of it as work—think of it as extortion." She laughed. The harsh laugh was softer, as if she were thinking of recent events between them.

"And don't think I won't come looking for a little, um, company every once in a while. I expect to get it."

Cord laughed. "Anything else? This is turning into quite a list."

"Don't worry. I'm saving you, Cord. I mean, I won't write your story yet. Don't know what I'll do with you yet. You're a terrific story. . . . First one I've ever put aside." A sadness swept across Chutney's face like black clouds across the Texas sky. "Here I am, not even thirty yet, and I'm already getting soft. How does a free-lance judge go soft?"

Cord shrugged.

Chutney's laugh pealed lightly through the Sacramento dampness. "You won't soften, right, Cord? Tough till the end."

"Congratulations once again, Captain Longborn," Chutney called as she took a couple of steps down the gangway. "I'll send you copies of the stories. I don't think you'll get rich on this river, but you seem to be the kind of person who knows how to keep things running efficiently. As long as you don't hit anything, that is." It was a bad joke and Jemima didn't laugh.

Chutney looked up at Cord and her eyes caressed his. "Good-bye, Mister . . . Diamondback. I trust you'll keep your skills in their fine state of tune." She slid a look at Jemima. Then back to Cord. "If you're ever in New York, get in touch. We can take a carriage ride around Central Park."

For a long moment, Chutney stared into Cord's face. Then she smiled at him softly before turning away.

"I'm ready. Let's go. I can't wait to get back to New York. I am *so* tired of mud, and dust—and above all I'm sick to death of steamboats." She sailed away, walking quickly to the bottom of the gangway. Then she stopped and turned.

"Best of luck to you, Mr. Diamondback. With your fights and your judging and all. Nice to know the West is in good hands." Again, the sarcastic laugh. Then she was gone, trailing Brake behind her like a dory.

Cord came back up the gangway.

Jemima looked up at him. "Your turn, Diamondback?"

"Soon."

"Hoodoo says you'd make a good river rat."

"Ships interest me," Cord said. "But not enough to make a life out of them."

Her wide mouth smiled, longing mixed with a little relief. "That's good, I guess. At least I don't have to worry about the competition."

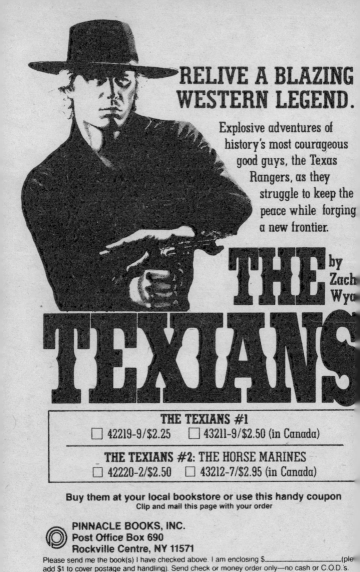